MIRA MARCINÓW (Szczecinek, 1985) is a writer and assistant professor at the Polish Academy of Sciences. *Queenless* is her fiction debut, for which she has received major Polish literary prizes: she was a laureate of the 2020 Polityka Passport in literature and a nominee for the Nike Literary Award in 2021. She has published three significant books on psychology. For her academic work, she was shortlisted for the Polityka Science Award in 2019 and won the Prime Minister's Award in 2015.

MAGGIE ZEBRACKA is a writer and translator from Chicago. A recipient of a 2021 National Endowment for the Arts translation grant, she holds an MFA in Creative Writing from Vanderbilt University and an MFA in Literary Translation from the University of Iowa, where she was an Iowa Arts Fellow. *Queenless* is her translation debut.

Mira Marcinów

QUEENLESS

TRANSLATED FROM THE POLISH
BY MAGGIE ZEBRACKA

HÉ/OÏSE

PRESS

First published in English in Great Britain in 2024 by
Héloïse Press Ltd
4 Pretoria Road
Canterbury CT1 1QL
www.heloisepress.com

Copyright © by Mira Marcinów, 2020
Originally published in Polish as *Bezmatek* by Wydawnictwo Czarne sp. z o.o., 2020

This translation © Maggie Zebracka, 2024

Majka Jeżowska, 'A ja wolę moją mamę' © Agat Passent, translated by Maggie Zebracka

Cover design by Laura Kloos
Edited by Mark Tardi
Text design and typesetting by Tetragon, London
Printed and bound in Great Britain by CPI Group (UK) Ltd, Croydon CRO 4YY

This publication has been supported by the ©POLAND Translation Program.

ISBN 978-1-7397515-9-3

This book is a work of fiction. Any resemblance to real-life characters, organisations, places and events is entirely coincidental.

BOOK INSTITUTE

©POLAND

QUEENLESS

Queenless – a honeybee colony without a queen.

I

One of my mother's lessons: use nail polish for runs in tights. Stops them from running further. If you have to wear nude tights, make sure they're cool-toned, to make the legs look slimmer. Warm tones fatten. And don't you dare let anyone find out that I'm this vain.

'I don't like you staring at me when I do my eyeliner. It makes my hands shake and then I have to start all over. You've always been fascinated by me doing my make-up. Girls usually are. Quit touching my back, it's distracting. And I don't really trust you, you know. That's how mothers are.'

Later, she drinks vodka and chases it with beer, becomes giddy and loud, dancing like Tina Turner. Other times, it makes her sad. She cries and smokes, tears and snot mingling on her Cupid's bow.

She seems so haughty, when she sits in front of me, my despondent mother, when she's hung-over and desperate for a drink and attempting to talk sincerely about the meaning of life, or when she's a few beers deep but she never once spanked me with a belt or interrogated me on Christmas Eve about my first time, or after the neighbours started gossiping about her, everyone convinced she wore gloves when washing dishes, like some non-mother, with her lacquered talons and other ornaments.

My grandma favoured housecoats, my mum was all about stilettos, leather pencil skirts, skin-tight blouses. That's how I remember her. She was one hundred and sixty-four centimetres tall, with chestnut hair and olive skin. The family even called her 'dark 'n' tall'. They'd tease her: 'Oh dear, how will you ever be dark 'n' tall, if you don't wear those heels?' Or: 'Of course, you have to walk with your nose turned up and stomach sucked in to be dark 'n' tall.'

Around strangers, she always added an extra centimetre. 'I'm one hundred sixty-five centimetres,' she said, straightening her posture. But she never did that around me.

I never saw her go to confession. I don't think she ever did.

Mum tells me that when I'm older, she'll pluck my eyebrows and then I'll be really pretty.

Even though we live in an apartment building – new, since it's from the '70s and it's only the '90s – we dream about living someplace else. Not in a quaint house with a garden, but in a large city. One day, we'll move to Szczecin. Mum says it's enormous. So huge that trains, which she says are called 'trams', criss-cross through it. There, you don't have to mind your neighbours and everyone lives how they please. Mum has already bought a figurine of a wild duck painted yellow and blue for our future kitchen, and some orange wooden eggs, too. There's nowhere to put them now. We live with my grandparents, who like dark, earthy tones and hues the colour of my skin. Generally, grandmothers prefer more melancholy places than mothers. Happy decor is allowed only in the big cities.

Mum fantasises about having her own kitchen. I dream of having my own room. One day, in our big city, we'll have a bachelorette pad – that's what they call apartments there. Mum is as pretty as Cindy Crawford, so she'll find work quickly and live in her own yellow-orange-blue kitchen, where she'll cook pasta with tomato paste and eggs. My favourite dish. Mum calls it 'rainbow pasta'. She rarely makes it now since this is my grandmother's kitchen. Every kitchen has her mistress. When two grown women share a kitchen, they're bound to argue. What matters most to my mum is the presentation of the food on the plate. But my grandmother only cares that you've eaten a lot of it. My mother's food is fragrant with spices I like smelling but not tasting. I'd like to have a red room with green dressers where I'll keep colourful embossed trading cards. But I know that there are no embossed cards, not really, even if you can imagine them when you close your eyes at night in bed.

My sister doesn't like the colour red, but Mum says she has to live with us until she's grown up. My sister has her own life. Even though she's only five years older than me, she's a serious person because she's already spending money. My sister steals hubcaps and sells them to someone in the neighbourhood. She claims she's already stolen a million rims but, really, it was a lot less than that, Mum says, and they were hubcaps, not rims. My mum, who is smart and good, doesn't allow us to steal.

What I'd most like to do with my mum is draw a duck beside her eggs, fill the whole sheet of paper with crayon. Leave no white spots, because Mum doesn't like them. It's not a real drawing if you can see through the paper, she says. What I'd most like is to be an artist, like her.

In the evenings, Mum washes her make-up off with soap. This, she lets me watch. She bends her head under the tap and scrubs her face. The water foams white. Mothers usually talk a lot when they're washing up. Mine, for example, reassures me that she's not going to lose her mind, which is the only time she looks like a Crazy Marta – that's what they call lunatics around here. But my mother isn't a lunatic. She's my mum.

'In our family, the women don't go grey,' my mum often said. She never got the chance to prove this herself.

She began the story of her childhood by telling me she had her first cigarette at the age of five. Huffing and puffing, you'd call it, not inhaling. Funny that she was fresh as a daisy. Still a baby. This was supposed to be amusing wordplay. I knew many people who laughed at her jokes.

She smoked like a dragon. When I woke each morning, she'd already burnt down a couple, sometimes even a dozen, cigarettes. It was how she measured time. I could tell when she'd got up by looking at the ashtray. Her fifth cigarette. Maybe seventh. Or tenth. But I couldn't always tell. I swept the butts into the trash twice. In better times, she smoked Marlboro Reds. Or Camels. Even the ones in the hard packs. *Hard cover* – top shelf. She hoarded those hard little boxes. Transferred cigarettes from the soft packs into them. In worse times, she smoked Karos, and in the worst of times, Klubowe. She claimed she'd never put the strong, filterless kind between her lips. But she did, when she had nothing better to smoke. When she was broke, she sent me to my grandma's for cigs. I made the rounds with the neighbours, too. In those days, a six-year-old with cigarettes in her fist was a normal sight. So I thought.

She stuck notecards to the fridge to track her smoking costs, converted to cars: 'I've smoked a Maluch's worth.' This was supposed to motivate her to quit. She sketched the Polski Fiat 126 next to it, but it didn't work because she didn't really like cars. To me, the message was clear: cars were for the rich, and if she hadn't been a smoker, we'd be rich. Later, she updated the card to: 'I've smoked a sedan's worth.' And she added a photo of a Polonez Caro. Eventually, it was just a picture of a car. Except she didn't even have a driver's licence. In the technical school, they'd made her get her tractor's licence, but apparently she never collected it. Maybe if she had drawn a house with a garden instead or at least an easel with her beloved Rembrandt brand oil paints, maybe then, on the 16th of March 2017, the anniversary of her diagnosis, it wouldn't have felt so natural for her to die.

People around us said that smoking kills, that cigarettes turn your fingernails yellow, your breath bad, and your teeth to rot.

They called her Lila – like something you might name a cat.

She knew she could always change her mind. But she never did.

Before she gained weight and became 'happy', she looked stunning, even with her early '90s teased fringe. Not everyone could pull it off. The same went for those thin black tights. Back then, only the lottery presenters wore them, their distorted, alien knees scaring the well-behaved children watching from home. My mother's legs, however, only looked human: lovely, slender, and appealing.

'The lottery drum has been emptied. The gate has been lifted. Let's start the pick-6 drawing.'

She thought she'd win the lottery one day. But she never did.

'Girls! Get my boots! We're going on a big shopping spree.'

'Really?'

'Yes, today's our lucky day. I can feel it.'

'Where are we going?'

'Turn on Polsat and turn up the sound!'

'But it's just commercials now.'

'Give it a minute! The lottery's about to start. Go on and grab the biggest bags we have while we wait.'

'Really? What're you going to buy? I'll take my backpack.'

Or it would be some promised bank transfer that never arrived. I remember that walk we took, suitcases in tow, for the great big shopping trip. I remember her sadness when she looked at me as we stood at the post office window. We always returned home with empty, sagging bags. It was extraordinary, how she let us dream.

She was getting on in years and wore capri pants, mint-green V-neck sweaters, and navy flats. People said her make-up was too heavy. I disagree. Everyone should be able to wear as much as they please. I feared her plunging necklines. And that she'd run out of money. She always had exact change, but often forgot that the cost of living was getting more and more expensive. Especially meat.

She liked looking good. She liked spending money on herself. She did look good, but had nothing to spend.

She used to work a lot. She was an animal care technician at a state-run farm, a receptionist at the Pomorski Hotel, a manager at the Słowianka sheltered workshop. After '89, she bought and sold steel and was great at it. She opened her own company. Went bankrupt. Tried to support her daughters on her own with an off-the-books job at Reich. Then took off. Was sent to a labour camp. Returned with broken ribs. In so much pain that I couldn't hug her. She looked for work. Didn't find any. Looked some more. She painted a few hundred large-scale portraits. Oil paintings. She sewed scraps of old leather clothes into artistic handbags that I sold to my college friends. We collected stones from the seaside for her brooches. She created miniature genre-scenes on them. Flat stones were the best: perfect for skipping, perfect for making money. Though she didn't make much.

'Remember, the most important thing is independence. Nothing's more disgusting for a woman than depending on others,' she said often.

And also:

'You need to have some sort of passion, and above all, get an education. No one can take that away from you.'

My mother was ashamed of a few things. Her teeth, her kitchen, and that she'd ended her studies but not her pregnancy.

Lila had three husbands. She changed her name after each wedding, for a total of four last names. She hadn't even reached sixty when she died. She had only daughters. My dad was her second. When I was seven, we moved to the apartment building across from my grandparents' to live with a man who wasn't my dad. The trade-off was that my mum had her own kitchen there. Three women with three different last names lived together in that new apartment. Sometimes even four, but by then, we'd fled from my mum's last husband to my grandma's. Having different surnames made many things easier. For instance, the question of who would kick off each game: who'd count first in Categories, who'd deal in Russian Schnapsen. We played alphabetically. You can, of course, go by first name, that's how normal families probably do it. But using our last names was more professional. And so Mum would start, then me, my grandma, and finally, my sister.

Those were the days when we lined our waste basket with newspaper. Very ecological of us. Except for the cigarette butts that clung to the sides, which would then need to be scrubbed clean. The days when we would ask, holding up a leathery bag: 'Is this derma?' Today, you'd call it 'eco-leather'. But 'derma' was more familiar then. Derma, from the Latin for 'skin'. What a fake language. So pretentious. In any case, this was back when all the doors in the apartment complex were wood panelling on one side and studded derma on the other. The entryways were panelled top to bottom with lacquered wood. Sheepskin rugs on the bedroom walls. Vinyl tiles on the ceiling. Those days.

Intensity reigned in our home. We adhered to the philosophy that, whenever possible, we should give ourselves up to excess. It was then that you abandoned truth. It was then that you truly lived.

In for a penny, in for it all – to use my stepfather's chirpy adage.

Lila had a fondness for the girls people gossiped about. She was one of them, after all. Despite doing everything that was expected of her. She had a job. She'd got married. Three times, even. She'd had children. Twice. She traded in her buzz cut for a modest bob. She bought her clothes from stores for mature women but lost not one bit of her allure. Everyone said that public opinion was important. But Lila gave the impression that she couldn't care less what people said.

You might assume that we talked about everything, did our nails together, chatted about sex. In any case, our relationship seemed like the sort.

But it wasn't.

I quickly find out from my older cousin that women in my family are temperamental in bed and that's why it's hard for them to find men. She talks about these issues with my mum, so she would know. I'm ten years old and I worry about my temper in bed. I've already heard that I have a bit of an attitude and because of this, my life will be no picnic. And now, this temper, too. Though my cousin seems proud when she tells me.

I'm wary of young men. But I'm even more fearful of the older ones. My grandfather, my mum's dad, wore a wifebeater: a striped white tank. And very short shorts. He poked out of them.

'Cover yourself up around the kids!' my grandmother would yell.

A huge snake. I haven't seen one like it since. He must have had some kind of medical condition, gigantism or something.

I was increasingly irritated by my mother's habit of narrating everything she did as she got older. She would talk to herself, but not because of dementia – she didn't live long enough for that. She was in her late forties when she began to whisper under her breath, 'Where's that dog bowl? I'm feeding him right now, yes, good, OK. Can't I have my coffee in peace for once? Kettle's on. Where'd I put that ashtray? No one's cleared the butts again! So many dishes! Does a whole army live here?' She talked to herself, just as her father had. My grandfather spoke to himself in the Zabużański dialect of the eastern borderlands, his words sounding like magic spells:

'Oj my bittle sack, why'd you give a tear?'

'Look, Kajtek!'

'Five years old I was, when I followed the cow.'

'Same in same out.'

'Job's your mother!'

When I was young, people who talked to themselves were crazy. That's pretty true today, too. Although this rule seems to evade mothers, since psychologists have said that a child's speech development can be hurried along by commenting on what you have just done. Playgrounds are filled with murmuring women chronicling their children's every move: 'Oh, now Kubuś has gone down the slide, now he's running, now he's tripped, and now he is looking at his mummy.' And so on in several languages. I prefer my mum – at least she was talking about herself to herself, not about me.

But I prefer my mummy,
with hair as black as ink,
and eyes golden like my teddy
when she cries into the sink.

But I prefer my mummy,
with hair as black as ink,
and eyes golden like my teddy.
She'll smile today I think.

Agnieszka Osiecka, 'But I prefer my mummy'

She returns laden with plastic grocery bags. Heaps of them. She doesn't know yet how harmful they are. She will not live to see pictures of plastic bags in the ocean, waves of bottles, flat fish with gaping mouths. She won't live to see the summer when everyone learns that the Earth has been suffocated with plastic. And the summer had been so beautiful that year.

My mother in heels. I hadn't yet realised how much harder it is to carry groceries with heels on. The weight distributes differently. Bunions form. In high heels, with bags full of chicken legs and barley groats, she looks beautiful. I would've been attracted to her, too.

She made her own pasztet from chicken skins. When she got them for free at the butcher's, she told the cashier they were for a dog. The chicken feet she gave to her bitch. The skins were for us. I adored this pâté.

'I made you pâté sandwiches for the road.'

Not that there was anywhere to go.

'I don't want to have sex where I have to imagine having sex.'

Wait, Mum. In grades one through three, I don't understand what this means. I know that when I'm grown and skinny, I'll get my period, then I'll have a teensy abortion, and eventually I'll have children, although I don't actually want them. This is the universal female experience. But now I don't want to hear about your fantasy.

Fantasy, fantasy, fantasy – fantasy takes you away

So you can play and play and play all day.
This mirror takes you everywhere
and it can show you anything.
Just hold it in your hand and stare,
and imagination will colour everything.
Just hold it, and it takes you there.
Add a pinch of fantasy, flair,
and you can rocket to the stars

Fantasy, fantasy, fantasies are for play

This mirror is never sad.
It always wants to smile.
It knows so many mysteries and will
be happy to help with everything.
Just take it in your hand,
add a pinch of fantasy and
you can run around the world with Mr Kleks!

Fantasy, fantasy, fantasy – fantasy takes you away

Fasolki, 'Fantasy'

My mother's words:

    'I don't think you remember who you're talking to.'

    'I'm your mother, not your friend.'

    'As long as you're living under my roof, I won't tolerate this kind of behaviour!'

    'You can say that to your friends, not to me.'

    'Go ahead, the door's wide open. Go. No one's keeping you here.'

    'Get out of my house!'

    'Who did I raise?!'

Also my mother's words:

    'You can tell me anything.'

    'You're my daughter and my best friend.'

    'How many times have you already saved my life?'

    'I don't deserve such a wonderful daughter.'

    'Why are you so good to me?'

    'I will always love you!'

    'When I grow up, I want to be like you!'

Her motherhood wasn't typical. Just like her cuisine. Watered down soup didn't bubble over in her pots. She would never allow it. If mothers can be reduced to the taste of their dishes, then we didn't have pork chops, but chicken in curry sauce. Even her special Christmas Eve pierogi were crispy brown dumplings with a rich, spicy mushroom filling. Nothing was ever bland. On the contrary, it was too spicy.

She liked mortadella with pistachios. She tried it in Tuscany and fell in love. Just like with the garlic-stuffed sausage, which we rolled up on the oilcloth-covered table in our microscopic kitchen.

'I don't know how much longer I'll live, but I'm going to keep eating this.'

'So what does your mother taste like?'
    'Spicy. But really, she's mellowed with age.'
    She always added less chilli to her children's dishes.

How can we not surrender to a woman between sixteen and forty-five years older, who claims to be related to us and seduces us with the words, 'I gave birth to you and wiped your arse. And this is how you thank me for it?'

It's hard not to give in to a tanned, well-made-up woman from whom we are separated by this ideal age gap.

Why are mothers so tanned?

After giving birth, they feel colder and have to bask in the sun, even if they don't like it.

Why do mothers wear so much make-up?

So that their daughters learn how to apply it themselves. Daughters should also pay attention to their mothers' make-up techniques for clues on how they want their post-mortem faces to look (mortuary cosmetology, post-mortem care – those things): from their make-up application while alive and from videos entitled 'Five Minute Make-up Tricks' or '19 Things You've Been Doing Wrong All Your Life', which says nothing about being an ungrateful daughter, but a lot about improperly arranging slices of ham on a square sandwich. (Slice two round pieces of ham in half and place them on the bread with the cut sides facing outwards. Problem solved.)

Yielding to your mother, becoming friends with her – it's bad business. She'll die before you. She'll abandon you. Hurt you. Pass. Let's not dance around it: our mothers will not be with us to the end. That isn't the natural order of things.

What are mothers like? Mothers are tired. Especially old mothers, dead mothers, and young mothers.

'Bat your eyelashes,' she often teased me.

I batted. I blinked. My eyelashes brushed her cheeks. It allowed me to be so intimate. She allowed me to go that far. You could say we were quite close. We were eye to eye with each other. Although at that time, my eyelashes were too long.

I started cuddling with her late, probably in my senior year of high school. Whenever she called me to her kitchen, I immediately ran to her, and she added:

'Tup, tup, tup, run to me with your little legs!'

I don't remember her saying that to me before.

I remember our first fight though. We returned to it often. It was about the *Kindergarten at Home* TV programme. About one fundamental question asked in the song that was difficult to understand. I thought it went like this: 'Where does the hedgehog stomp at night? You can find out, if you want.'

But my mum insisted that the children sang 'Where does the hedgehog stare at night?'

Today, you can fact-check this yourself, browse internet memes of hedgehogs with captions like, 'We know where the hedgehog stomps at night' or 'Who are we, where are we stomping?'

I was right.

But nothing comes of it.

I thought that I couldn't go any further, any deeper in experiencing my own life. No further than my mother.

'Someday, you'll grow up to be who you really are.'

That's what my mum and primary school teacher told me. I heard it from someone else, too. I don't remember who. But I never understood it. I knew it was good that I would grow up to be human. Except I wasn't sure why I wasn't considered one already. Maybe because not everything was the same with us as with others? In fact, it was too much. Too much, because until I went to school I didn't know my father, and my sister didn't know hers, because we had different fathers and built fantasies around them. Too much, because there was nothing to eat. And it was freezing in our apartment block in the winter after they installed meters on the radiators. Too much, because Grandpa beat Grandma. Too much, because Grandma still mourned the death of her son, who'd hanged himself. Too much, because my mum drank, gained weight, and cried.

About her suicidal younger brother, she said:

'He was insatiable, forever wanting more, always wanting to be first. He even tried death before I could. Paweł wanted to beat me to everything.'

And me, she advised:

'Remember that you've earned everything yourself.'

And:

'You can eat or drink your way through money, but you have to live through life.'

'Those who eat fast, work fast' – she claimed this was from Fellini's *La Strada*.

She ate standing up, as mothers do, asking how I liked what she'd made, while the food passed through her lips, unchewed, untasted.

'Those who eat leftovers are gorgeous and smooth all over.'

'I'll eat it. I don't want it going to waste.'

And again:

'There are no pigs in our house.'

She ate what the picky eaters left behind.

Other times, she would say:

'No one has died from bad smells, but many from draughts.'

She delivered these pseudo-sayings charmingly, with a smile, especially the last one. That's how we talked. We still managed to joke about it all.

She sautés and sautés, using only sunflower oil. Bakes and bakes, but only meat. Cakes are for other, more submissive women. What is it like to spend your evenings pondering what to put in the pot the next day? I don't know. She did the thinking. Meanwhile, I fell asleep imagining what I'd wear to school. Not because of poverty, but pure imagination.

We had our song. She taught it to me. We'd hold hands, dance greedily. Mum sang, or rather, chanted loudly:

'Mother! Afterwards, no strength remains. Her body's got flabby.'

'Why?' That was my line, delivered with all the drama of a cabaret actress.

To which Mum sing-songed, 'She tears the blood out from her veins. She does it for her baby.'

For years I thought she made it up, that the song somehow was hers. But recently I discovered the original:

> Mother every night must drink.
> She lingers on the dance floor.
> Because she has a child she thinks
> She has someone to live for.
> Afterwards, no strength remains.
> Her body's got flabby.
> She tears the blood out from her veins
> She does it for her baby.

A song from Janusz Morgenstern's film
See You Tomorrow, performed by the Bim-Bom Theatre

Our song.

At least for me, the road to my mother was closed, and it was raining.

My mother painted. When one painting of hers was still far from finished, I could see it was of a pillow set on a windowsill. To paint a pillow in this place suggested an onlooker. We lived directly across from the apartment of my mother's mother. Something might have happened in the channel between our blocks. Many watched just as we did. But for some reason, we felt superior to those women resting their elbows on their pillows. We watched life in the apartment blocks discreetly. Through our green blinds, we watched as autumn died and then as other, lesser seasons kicked the bucket.

We painted still lifes together. Mum posed a bottle, next to it a vase and a little plate. Then she handed me and my sister a cup of water for our paints. For as long as I can remember, I've been afraid of still lifes.

My mum had a philosophy about the art of living. The smallest things made her happy. She saw the beauty in inanimate objects. That's how she was able to decorate our forty-eight-square-metre apartment in the ugly '70s apartment block, give it ambience. Most people don't know how to be content with the lives they're dealt, with lives that reflect their worst fears. She could. She was the first to show me how.

She spent every morning at the table by the kitchen window. That's where she drank and smoked, cried and did her make-up, where she told me everything, but nothing about herself. She admitted to as many betrayals as she could. She wasn't able to admit to all of them – the alcohol made her forgetful.

The kitchen was burdened with everything. The tea-coloured lace curtains stained with smoke, the shattered bottles beneath the table, the pile of butts in the brushed gold, leaf-shaped ashtray. The scents of home: cigarettes, vodka, pickle brine, oil paints, garlic curry, fixative.

For twenty-five years. She lived a quarter century with her last husband before she died.

Grandparents were supposed to be the first to die, of course. Followed by the parents of our friends and relatives. And only after, could you expect this.

There ought to be some order to death.

When she was late returning home, I went on high alert in the apartment after dusk. Perched in the kitchen, at the table near the window. Lights out. Nose pressed to the glass. The curtain raised and secured with a hair tie to keep it up. The blinds raised, too, for a better, quicker view. Sometimes, I would open the door and sit in the dark entryway, listening for footsteps. I loved the click of her heels on the stairs, especially when her steps were brisk, sharp, even. When the sound was muddled, I knew I had to race down to the ground floor, often in just my socks. Swaying steps sound off. The heels ring against the concrete differently. Sometimes, you had to help her get inside. When I propped her up, she fell more frequently. As if she felt safer. Without me, she somehow managed to stay upright.

I'll never forgive you for being late, I thought. But when she sobered up, like the prodigal son, I loved her even more. We never found the time to talk about these anxieties during her absences.

The fear of her dying had always been with me. I knew how it would happen. When she disappeared for a few days, her sister said that my mum was probably lying under the snow. Drunk. Without her underwear. She'd fallen asleep. She'd freeze. I knew she'd die in late winter and we'd find her only in the spring. The first part came true.

And just like back then, staggering on those stairs, I still worried about her. It was only much later that I learnt how to deal with this. When I left for college, I never called her at night. Or even in the afternoons. This narrowed my risk of hearing her drunk, honest, despairing. I usually called her first thing in the morning or around noon. We'd talk for a long time. She was safe. I was safe.

I can't talk about this.

She said: 'you'll chicken foot your toes' (and I chicken footed them, meaning I slotted my fingers between them); 'gather up the house' (I gathered it, meaning cleaned, but kind of half-arsedly); 'rub the potatoes' (I grated them). She used many regional eastern dialects.

Mum sat in the kitchen in the mornings, sipping her Turkish coffee in silence. Suddenly, her strangled cry:

'No use sitting around. Have to get to work! No one's gonna do it for me!'

It was after seven, the morning fog above the Tesco dissipating in the cold air. My mother was already hauling pots onto the stove. She complained about my room, where she stored her easels. There, peering at her latest painting, she burnt down another cigarette. She checked to see if the oil paint had dried enough for another layer. She smoked, stared and a Mona Lisa smile sketched itself on her face. She looked fulfilled. At that point, she wasn't working anymore. But she laboured over herself like a bull.

She tidied, she poured, another day survived.
  Mum wept.

The story of our ancestry changes each time she tells it. In one, the Tatars who raped my great-grandmother were responsible for my dark eyes. Their colour caused her problems when she was divorcing my dad and her mother-in-law said that no one in her family had eyes like that – and my mum's eyes are green, my dad's blue. In another, we're Jews or my grandmother's brother was shot along with his wife and son for sheltering two Jewish women they knew from college.

But we're rarely, if ever, Russian. They only say that about us because of our accent. In my mother's papers, it says: 'Place of birth: USSR'. She insists they made a mistake, because where she's from, Poles lived. I was born in the Republic of Poland, but I have a drawl. Kids at the playground laugh at me, because I sound like the singer Czesław Niemen. And he sings for old and sad people.

In all the versions, we're mixed. That's why it's so difficult for us. But Poland is important, even if they don't like us here, because our grandparents died for Poland. And now we can speak Polish. In any case, if not for my grandparents, we wouldn't be able to speak Polish in Poland. We would've had to learn foreign languages, which is very difficult and expensive. We can't afford it. That's what I thought then.

My mother didn't allow me to use pronouns when talking about her.

'I'm not some "she" to you. I'm your mother.'

Every Sunday at ten, she turned on Polsat for her daughters. The show *Disco Relax,* thanks to which the Poles managed their hangovers. We danced to Shazza's 'Want It, Take It' and sang with Casablanca:

> Oh mum, oh mum, oh mum,
> I'm in love with a gypsy.
> I want to be a gypsy
> who dances with the dawn.

Nothing racy. Pure joy in the morning. Still in our pyjamas with our beloved, warm, a lightly tipsy mum. We had a television then. We even had cable. We had it good. I was in Year 5 when I learnt from my mother that in life, what counts is what a person knows and what they've lived through and not what they had. We played disco polo behind drawn curtains, but we talked about books. I knew that Dostoyevsky was a great writer. But I was really captivated by my mother: she danced funny, sang even funnier, read difficult writers, and knew even more difficult words.

'Mum, mum, say the weird word again?'

'Deoxyribonucleic acid.'

'Wow! Demoxyrimonulonyk? ... Ugh, I can't. Say it again, mum?'

She was the source of my greatest happiness just as today she is the source of my greatest sorrow.

'One beautiful childhood memory and you've been redeemed.'
If that's true, then my mother saved me.

Sometimes, she went on Sunday walks with her young daughters. Singing *Parasolki* by Koterbska together while soldiers whistled at her from the barracks. In the summer at the lake, when she readied herself and dived head first from the dock in her one-piece swimsuit, the men shouted strangely. And asked Mum out for dinner. She wore a one-piece because of the scar I'd given her. A scar from her daughter. Horizontal, C-section. Meanwhile, my scar from my mother – my belly button – wasn't worthy of navel-gazing, wasn't any centre of the world, though I acted like it was.

No one could talk back like her, reacting so non-flirtatiously to cat calls.

My mother must have been so beautiful!

Green eyes and a smile that glows
and two shoes on her feet and yellow freckles on her nose
and all the people can't suppose
how I can't eat, can't rest,
forget her for a second at best.
Olé, olé, olé, olé
We won't give in, we won't go away
Olé, olé, olé, olé,
We won't give in, we won't go away.
The score is four to none, Wielim puts the losers on the run,
my only football club,
and all the people can't suppose
how I can't eat, can't rest,
forget her for a second at best,
Olé, olé, olé, olé etc.

From a recovered memory of a football chant remixed with my
stepfather's drunken song about my mother

She loved me as she could in her maternal way. Though it always seemed to me that she loved me more than that.

She could appreciate kitsch.

'Every home should have a bit of kitsch,' she said. 'It helps create a living space. Instead of a photo from an interior design magazine.'

Mum was a regular reader of *Your Style* and *Four Corners*. Before that, *Success* and *Burda*. She took pride in having read *Profile*. Compared to the other apartments at that time, we had a good number of books. One wall unit. When I read *Your Style*, I asked my mother many questions.

'What does "anomaly" mean?'

Mum patiently explained. Or she told me to check the encyclopaedia, reminding me she wouldn't 'be around forever'. I jotted the definitions down in my diary. I didn't have a mind for memorising new words.

Now I remember. The room is warm and dry. The cobalt blue wicker basket holds a few art books. Just like in Mum's beloved *Four Corners*.

These were the better times, when Mum brought home books as thick as my thighs. Imposing, lying open on the coffee table. When I was little, Mum always put her feet up on the coffee table. And then Book World was founded. Albums with glossy pages and hard covers were delivered to our house. I remember that among them was *The Complete Prophecies of Nostradamus*. At home, we also had a collection of Russian books, short stories rather than huge tomes. Dostoyevsky's *White Nights*, Tolstoy's *Stories and Novels*, of which I best remembered 'Three Deaths'.

We argued about books. She mocked my weakness for *Paradise* by José Lezama Lima, for his baroque prose. Later, she apologised. She loved Márquez's *One Hundred Years of Solitude*. (I never understood this and never apologised for it.) I slipped her Henry Miller. And Anaïs Nin, whom she never took to. Nin was too shifty for her, unreliable. The kind who appears out of thin air in the rain, with a green umbrella and polka dot dress. The kind she believed led her twenty-one-year-old younger brother to hang himself.

The repo man comes knocking. Mother and daughter pretend they're not home. They're playing hide and seek. Open up please. Playtime stops. In walks the repo man, or social services, or some other dick/cunt. Though I'm young, I understand that I'm allowed to hate them, but they don't get to humiliate us. I don't grasp what this means. Only that it's unfair. People are bad and want to hurt us. Family is the most important. Though not ours. Sometimes I'm the worst. Worse than my grandma, my aunt, and even my dad. You're just like your father. Now that I'm older, I've learnt to talk back. I'm mouthy, sullen, a smart aleck. Except it wasn't me who married him, it was you. My father is a drunk and a thief, and also completely indifferent towards me. They separated when I was born, so it's all my fault. My fault, my fault, my most grievous fault. This is my confession.

When I went to the mental health clinic the first time – I was about fifteen years old then – the doctor said: 'The crux of the issue is that your mother is your child.'

It lasted some three months before my mum's business went bankrupt. But what a time that was! All the sweets, the people, the alcohol. The Polonez Caro from the showroom. After, we had to scrounge just to find something to eat.

Summers were easier. Abandoned yards around the apartment blocks, with potatoes as small as strawberries. Thatches of wild strawberries as small as blueberries. A bit of dill. Wild sorrel. Yellow plums. A grocery bag full of vegetable peel. 'Bin-diving' – my favourite slang word from 1998. I stole from backyards, pretending to be looking for my grandmother or grandfather. Caught red-handed, I said that I lived in the poorhouse. Nobody would have given me even one little apple if I told them I lived with my mother and stepfather in an apartment block, like a normal person, like them. Mum baked biscuits with the pilfered apples. With a strong aftertaste of one-złoty margarine. I appreciated this. Biscuit-baking was for ordinary mothers; the artistic ones made spicy dishes, adult dishes, as we called them. But she made an exception for me. Margarine, slack-baked, stolen apples. The taste of summer '98. I long for it.

This was all a long, long time ago, when the world was omni-present with joy and mothers never died.

There was no fridge, no washing machine, no TV, the desk also had to be sold, and there were no toys. But we kept the coffee table. The bread slicer, too. It's important. It can slice the bread very thinly. Especially when it's stale. We struggled more with the lack of clothes, but grandma had many old housecoats and belts. Grandma was rich because she always had something to eat with bread. Smoked mackerel with mayonnaise and onion, cottage cheese with sour cream and pasztet. She had a pension, supposedly the lowest amount you could get, but she was probably just being modest.

Poverty kept me slim during my teenage years, while many of my friends were gaining weight. But it also stunted my growth. I didn't outgrow my parents, I didn't outgrow anyone. Not even my stoop-shouldered grandmother, who shrinks with each passing year. Besides, for dancers, which I wanted to become, being too tall is a curse.

The school required insurance – we didn't pay for it. Apparently the parents of other students donated to a fund for the poorest among us. In high school, I was the poorest, the only one. I turned up my nose. I did homework during the breaks between classes with borrowed textbooks because I didn't have my own. When I received money for books and clothing, I spent it on trips to Krakow – the city of artists, as I saw it then. I bought a red corduroy coat, orange bovver boots, a colourful striped cardigan, and a little purse on a chain, which promptly broke.

Why didn't we have any money? Because we didn't cheat, we didn't steal, we had no connections, we didn't belong to the party. Even though my grandfather told my mother to draw Lenin, a beautiful collection of minor communist saints took his place, as part of my mother's painting project from the age of seven. I don't know how I understood why some people were poor. But it was obvious to me: poverty affected the good, the noble, the honest, the sensitive. Or the disabled, like the Brzezińskis from the apartment at the end of the hall. The rich were suspect. There was nothing to envy about them. Maybe this was my mother's way of protecting me from feeling inferior?

We belonged to families that, in the flush times of Pewex and Pepco, could not afford toys for their children.

I never called her 'tired'. She tried. I've said this many times. She tried so hard. As mothers did. Only more so.

When a mother and daughter love each other this much, it's frightening to be near them. Frightening to die. *Love Story*. A romantic comedy. I'd watch it. A beautiful mother meets her brilliant daughter, and they fall in love. But they don't realise it yet because it's an enemies-to-lovers scenario. A heartwarming family movie. Light, sunny. With a strong female lead. #yourworld

One night, she took us sledding. Me, my sister, and our two cousins. There was a bitter frost. Unlike the ones we have now. We climbed the highest hill in the area. My sister and cousins slid down the hill with my laughing mother. I was afraid. For myself, but also for her. Even then, I knew I was missing out on the simple joy of carefree fun. That night, my mother broke her arm. Mothers don't break their arms while sledding, that's what I thought then. We waited until morning to see a doctor, to avoid her being sent to the hospital drunk tank, told to sleep it off.

My mother was the source of my greatest happiness. And my greatest sorrows.

A young, tipsy mother is suspicious.

Her daughters must become the guardians of her virtue.

Nights are difficult.

Darkness. A chubby baby writhes in the sheets of the marital bed. The mother lies near the edge. The neckline of her housecoat gapes to her navel. It doesn't cover anything. The baby's fish mouth latches onto one nipple. The second one is subject to a palpating exam. No woman wants to do such things to her own nipples. She looks at the baby greedily juggling her breasts. It leers at them. Hatred, despair, love. She finally pulls its lips and fingers from her body. But it doesn't matter anymore. Because the daughter wakes up.

Sunrise.

Mornings with a child are punctuated with strangeness. The little milkfucker peers from behind the breast. Seduces you within seconds of waking.

This morning, the breasts have produced no milk. She leisurely pressed her thumb above the nipple and cupped the fleshy underside in her palm. This is how she usually activated the fountain. The time of spontaneous ejaculation has long passed. Not without a hand, without a child. The stream diverts immediately from the milky way to the digestive tract. Its colour, therefore, is rarely described. It resembles the liquid squeezed from a damp sponge after wiping a blackboard. Chalk and water. Drawing and erasing combined in milk created for other purposes. She stares at droplets of a different colour. This morning, what flowed from her chest was paint.

My favourite thing is to lie face down outside.

The earth smells of rain, my mother, and something else.

It's good to be with Mum at home,
both in sunlight and the gloam.
We throw a red ball back and forth.
After, she will draw a cat
and give me sweet chocolate.
She must know fairy tales, hours' worth.

It's good to be with Mum at home,
both in sunlight and the gloam.
Her anger can burn like a hearth,
but when you're hurting she appears
to soothe your cries and wipe your tears.
She knows her fairy tales, hours' worth.

The opening titles of the *Mum and Me* show

We could have changed the world, flaunted our crazy mother-daughter love and proved that life within this configuration makes remarkable sense. Yet we didn't do that. She hardly left the house. Only short trips to Biedronka. Or to pay the bills after the first or tenth of the month. I don't remember exactly which day my stepfather received his pension. People let her down, especially women. She never counted on men, at least not for as long as I can remember. That is, since she was thirty.

At that moment, I realised that at around the age of thirty, I too fell into a similar trap: I stopped leaving the house and decided that if I didn't do something in the morning, I probably wouldn't get to it at all. I decided I had zero energy after eleven o'clock. My outings were limited to quick morning grocery runs to the shop next door. I put make-up on for this occasion, donned my armour. Our lives, mine and my mother's, became unbearably mirrored. My mother, like me, limited her social life to her immediate family. She smiled too much and looked unnatural, fake – like me, I'm afraid.

I wanted a bolder life than my mother's. I wanted one more daring.

I called her every day. I was ashamed of this. I began travelling abroad for longer periods of time, as if to rehab. Because it was prohibitively expensive to make long-distance calls. International calls. But even in New York, I would go to Starbucks daily and we would Skype.

Yes, I was dependent on my mother. After our conversations, I felt hung-over. But I couldn't stop myself. I needed her to be the source and witness of my life. A loyal fan: critical, inspiring, argumentative. I was worried that because of me, she had no life of her own, instead squeezing her existence in between our calls. When I didn't call, she was furious. After a one-day break, she reproachfully asked:

'What are you calling me for?'

She liked that she was my heroin. I liked to believe that she was addicted to me, too. Meanwhile, my guilt grew.

'Live your own life!'

Or rather, 'You have to learn how to live your own life!'

That's what she said. But was that what she wanted?

Ours was a very unhealthy family.

I list her flaws. What good is it? I'm trying to grow disgusted with my mother. She wasn't that great, after all. I wasn't that in love with her, after all. I didn't love her that much.

How I love her, this mother of mine!

Mother – a highly addictive substance.

During her lifetime, I wound up in rehab many times. I wanted to learn how to live without her. Without any addictions. I didn't last long. Two or three days tops.

And now – complete abstinence.

She told me about herself in front of me, about Lila, who, before she got pregnant, roamed around barefoot and braless, shaved her head bald in her small town, and tattooed a peace sign on her left wrist with a needle. She showed me the scars. So many legends.

She narrated the whole story from the beginning many times, as though she had never told it before.

I knew that if we drank together, I'd get to know her better. So we shared pulls from a bottle of cheap red wine. Always off-season on the beach in Mielno. It drizzled. And we got drunk. We danced in the dunes. We sang hits by Doda and Ich Troje, 'Colours of the Wind' by Edyta Górniak, from *Pocahontas*. The repertoire of Kayah and Bregović was a suitable addition. I kept falling over and dragging my giggling mother down with me. We roared with laughter. Pissed our pants. My mother probably more so after two pregnancies. Our Kegel muscles have betrayed us more than once.

That night in the dunes, with both of us drunk, I no longer feared for her when she drank alone. When I had vowed to never drink alcohol, I said: I will never drink. And again: There's nothing worse in the world. And before I went to sleep I prayed:

> Angel of God, my guardian dear,
> To whom God's love commits me here,
> Ever this day, be at my side,
> To light and guard, rule and guide.
> Amen.

And to this I added:

> And help me; make my mum and stepdad stop
> drinking.

Or I thought about the absent father, saying:

> Demon of shadows, my watcher near,
> To whom God's disdain confines me here,
> Ever this night, lurk by my side,
> To obscure and haunt, control and misguide.
> The end.

The road to my mother is long and exhausting. You have to change trains in Poznań. Or Piła. And still, there might be delays.

My mother didn't really care about her role as a good parent.
This made it easy for me to love all of her. The whole mother is:
    playful mother
    concerned mother
    single mother
    Polish mother
    harried mother
    painter mother
    unemployed mother
    ungrateful mother
    conscientious mother
    warm mother
    heroic mother
    fucked-up mother
    fashionable mother
    sleeping mother
    drunk mother
    bare-faced mother
    sober mother
    husbandly mother
    adulterous mother
    fantastical mother
    scandalous mother
    local mother
    my mother
    your mother
    nobody's mother

or have I already told you about the time Paweł and I set a mobile phone on fire and the fire department came, and Dad, your grandfather, beat us with a belt, but we were afraid, I was probably five years old, I've probably already told you the story of how we stole cabbages from the Chelises, and how they chased us and I was laughing the whole time, I don't think I've ever told you, that Paweł nearly drowned in the swamps, even then I knew that he was pulled towards death, I was never pulled towards it, but I died anyway

2

On the day my mother began to die, I drank a cappuccino at Bunkier Sztuki and a caramel latte at Tektura. I bought pastries made with black cumin.

Maternal care procedures: washing up, changing nappies. I didn't want to do it wearing gloves. There is a joke repeated by proctologists regarding a rectal exam: no gloves for VIPs. And that's how I treated my mother. My Very Important Person.

'Do you want me to die?'
    'I'd rather you didn't, Mum.'

The Magnificent Century is playing in my mother's room at the radiotherapy ward in Rydygier Hospital. A Turkish period drama about the life of Sultan Suleiman the Magnificent. You have to pay five złoty to turn on the TV. There are three cancer patients in the room, all women. They often cry when yet another beautiful Ottoman princess succumbs to cancer. One of the patients is bald and ravenous: she noisily devours Cheetos, cheesy spirals. After everything, these will become my favourite snack. My mother doesn't want to watch the TV, turns her gaze towards the window. We are on a high floor, the fifth I think. The sky is leaden. Nowa Huta. This is not a room with a view.

Hospital life goes on around her, someone argues about the coffee from the machine and its superiority over coffee from the cafeteria, someone is opening another bag of crisps, but she is silent. I'm afraid of the grimace on her face. But I'm also impressed by her refusal to give in to the mindless chatter, that she maintains her dignity.

She wasn't one to complain. Nothing disgusted her more than talking to complainers. At the butcher's – complainers. She proudly bought bones, said: 'A few bones for my dog, please,' and made soup for us with them. At the oncology ward – complainers. She was dying there, with no chance of recovery, no prospect of surgery or cutting something out that might come back later. That's what my proud mother did. What else was she proud of? Her Tatar roots. A bit less of the Jewish ones, because of her relationship with her mother. That the women in our family were fighters. From Aunt Maria, who went with Anders' army to Monte Cassino. To me. That's what she said. But that's what all parents tell their children.

Please insert five złoty.

I recently read somewhere that 'Love means telling someone: you won't die.' I had to tell my mother: 'You will die. You will die soon.' And I've never loved anyone more.

Was it her fault she was dying? Was it mine? Someone else's? The cigarettes'? Her lungs'? Was it because of her curiosity about the other world over this one? Was it because of the lack of medication for metastatic small cell lung cancer? Which had sown itself in her:

> kidneys;
> lymph nodes;
> liver;
> lungs;
> bronchi;
> brain and cerebellum.

The poppies the old woman was sowing, she did so without knowing, the grandfather knew, but his voice never grew, though already the cancer was showing, the cancer knew, too, but didn't say boo, now this is how it's going:

I liked to please my mother, a mama's girl. A mother undergoing chemotherapy has cravings: she has an appetite while on steroids, so I buy her shrimp in a wine-butter sauce, and I order grilled salmon with sweet potato, and a meringue cake.

This was our ritual. After each stay at the infusion centre, after each chemo session, I asked my mum to join me for ice cream at the Słodki Wentzl pastry shop. On the corner of the Main Market Square and Grodzka Street in Krakow. And while we waited to be admitted to the hospital, we visited a café. Each time a new one: a table in the courtyard garden at Mehoffer's, Dynia, Mięta, Bonjour Çava, Tektura, Karma. Krupnicza Street in Krakow – cancer street.

There is nothing more hideous in this world than when a person dies on another person.

When an animal dies on another animal.

Mum had shingles, then cancer. It's easy to imagine. First, shingles slithers in, and then cancer muscles inside, pincers clacking. I naïvely thought that shingles always preceded cancer. I've had shingles three times since my mother's diagnosis. Meanwhile, people say that you only get shingles once in your life. And also that you only live once. It's terrible, the things people say.

Five things you should do with a mother dying of cancer:

1. Go out often for ice cream/coffee/wine/vodka/a joint/ salmon/pastry/shrimp.
2. In case of brain metastases: remember that you're dealing with an adult woman.
3. Forgive or apologise.
4. Spend as much time together as possible. No 'quality time' either. Watch TV together, people-watch, hold hands. Be bored often.
5. Have a heart-to-heart about the fact that she is dying.

Apparently, cancer exposés are written to sell something. What could my mother's lung cancer be selling? Breast cancers are women's cancers; lung cancers are gender-neutral.

From the *Kindergartener's Workbook*: 'Where doesn't a crab live: in the sea, in your sink, in a shell?'

Well, my mother's crabby cancer was lurking in her kitchen after all.

I gave a lecture to philosophy students about the Hollow-Mask illusion. For an hour and a half, I misspoke many times, each time referring to the Hollow-Mum illusion instead. Mask – mum. The thing about the Hollow-Mask illusion is that faces are convex. When a mask representing a human face is concave, our mind makes it convex. Because we see these more often. Only people with schizophrenia can see that the mask is concave. Just as the Romantics wanted: only a madman sees the truth.

My mother was concave. She was dying. There were those who were under the illusion of her concavity. On steroids, which reduced the tumour in her brain, she possessed more of these bodily concavities. But schizophrenia has made me immune to this illusion. From the beginning of my mother's illness, I saw that the mask was concave, I knew that my mum was dying, I had no illusions to the contrary. My mother is simply dying. Dying. Dying. Dying.

I'm repeating what is said in similar situations. Few people can clearly define dying. It turns out that I can't. I clumsily tell my mother that she is dying. I'm not very good at this part. If it was taught in schools and tested, I don't know if I'd even get a C. Maybe I'd even fail. Did I fail to try hard enough?

Three hundred and sixty-five days from diagnosis to death. I tried not to look away, to look my mother straight in the eyes. But I couldn't always do it. Actually, I don't know if I truly succeeded even once.

She was not of dying age. How do I know this? Because if my mother were famous, journalists wouldn't have written an advance obit for her yet. The writer Jacek Dehnel says that this is what they call posthumous articles submitted to the editor in advance, these 'toe tag' bios. For the potentially dead, famously advanced in years. They are completed before the day of their actual death. I didn't even start writing anything like my mother's 'toe tag' in my journal. I've been writing about my grandmother for a long time. I regularly add new diseases, because my grandmother has been dying for as long as I can remember. My mother had slightly chilled feet at best. I massaged her feet. She said they hurt, 'Give me a massage', she said. There was something Christian about it. Washing and massaging someone's feet, and other gestures of suffering whose symbolism I hated.

She was dying. At an early age. At an age not yet advanced. Maybe this is actually the dying age?

It's taken me a long time to understand that it's impossible to fill every moment of life with maximum tension. And that it's not worth doing.

At first, my mother fell. Thwack, crack, and cancer. And yet, something like a savour of life. At the same time that I was taking care of my mother, I had a busy nightlife. Actually, not really. In one text message, I cancelled a meeting, using the excuse that my mother was dying. In a second one, I arranged a little trip to the bar at the same time: 'Want to get a beer?' I pretended that my mum was undergoing chemotherapy so as not to have to explain myself. I was putting my mother to sleep in the nursery.

My mother was dying in my daughter's room. During this time, my husband and I made love faster and faster. Before midnight, I'd look into the next room. She was breathing loudly, suffered from bruxism, ground her teeth. I've inherited this from her. She coughed occasionally. I didn't know yet how she would breathe near the end. I just assumed she wouldn't die quietly. It wouldn't be a sudden death, but rather its opposite. Another time I came back in the morning. I cleaned up after her. Expressed milk. Fed my daughter. Fed my mother. I didn't sleep. I lied.

When my mother was dying, I tried to hide the difference between us. I have never been as numb to death or as ready to live as when she was dying. I did what other people did. Even more so. How could I just fall in love, drink, and dance while she was suffering in the next room? She couldn't do what

I could, and around her, I pretended that I couldn't do it either. But I could and I did. I thought then that I wouldn't live without her. We were supposed to die together, but I'm alive. I just feel a little deadened, Mum.

Mothers, like villains, require tenderness.

I believe you must have a talent for dying. My mother talked about dying with impressive sincerity. I don't know if you can maintain emotional coherence when talking about your suddenly impending death. But I know she could. To share it in a way that meant we died together. Even though I can't quote her words, I know they came true. I know they hurt. However, I remember her strange screams. When – what's the saying? – she wasn't 'all there', she shouted: 'Moccasins for a jacket!' Then cried. Her face drawn with sadness and disappointment. Because I didn't understand her, my mother.

'Moccasins for a jacket, moccasins for a jacket, moccasins for a jacket, moccasins for a jacket,' I keep telling myself. I still don't know. I don't think she'd ever used the word 'moccasins' in front of me before. I doubt she ever wore moccasins. A jacket's another story. Maybe she still wanted to go somewhere?

When I was little and my mum cried, I would tell her: 'Don't cry, or I'll cry, too.' We cried together. When I was thirty-one, I said to her: 'Don't die, or I'll die, too.' But as you know, that didn't happen.

Nothing could have happened during the year my mother was dying. Cancer stole her strength. There were no third-act twists. Only lying and waiting for death.

Somehow I couldn't get myself together. Or worry the right amount or enter a depressive state.

The wheelchair sat next to the pushchair like a pretentious installation about the passage of time. XXL adult nappies next to size 5 premium nappies. I squeezed myself between these pushchairs in the hall and understood the banality of their literal nature. I felt tight.

Death – let's escape it by the sea! Let's snort cocaine! Let's have sex without having to imagine sex!

It was my mother who deeded me a love for life, which was confused – both in her and me – with a fascination with men. And women. At least in my case. I don't know that about her. Was my mother also attracted to women? How could I check?

I never told my mother about my lust for the younger girl. Or about the woman with bright eyes and thick skin, the kind where you can't see the veins, different from mine. With full lips, like my mother's, who told me my lips would grow bigger.

'Mine looked like yours when I was your age.'

'Mum, my lips won't grow anymore, lips don't grow after thirty. That's your long-running joke on me.'

I could go on and on about lips. I love kissing, have kissed various women's lips, even those made of silicone, rubber, those sticky with bubblegum lip gloss, and rouged with Chanel lipstick smelling of grandmothers.

Mother!
Afterwards, no strength remains.
Her body's got flabby.
Why?
She tears the blood out from her veins
She does it for her baby.

These two events should not be happening at the same time under the same roof: the infancy of my first child and cancer, followed by the death of my mother. So I naïvely thought.

I exploited my social attractiveness for an important anti-cancer purpose. Something cracked and I spilt myself into all sorts of young men and even younger women. Talking, flirting, manipulating. As if I had to make up for all those years when she would no longer be with me. I wanted to know her reactions to 'I'm going to have a son' or the even more pretentious 'I'm quitting academia.' The career that had showed so much promise.

All the while, a gangbang in my head.

Sex – the best rebuttal to death's ultimatum. When a loved one dies, the fucking justifies itself.

An oncowhore is a person who has sex in exchange for a cancer treatment for a loved one or, less often, for themselves. An oncowhore uses their sexuality to get medical care when doctors offer a terminal diagnosis. In this way, they attempt to extend the life of a family member by a year, by lakes, by their granddaughter's first words, by seafood.

'Could this be your perverse defence during psychosis?' asks a psychoanalyst acquaintance.

Perverse because instead of thinking about dying, you think about sex.

This happens sometimes.

Perverse because some promise oncological treatment in exchange for sex.

It happened to me.

Retrospection is a trap.

I have bad and strange memories from this time. I can only compare it to those rare moments when we are exceptionally sad and calm, when we try to be present despite everything, when we alternately get closer to reality and move away from it so much that it makes us want to puke.

The last quarter of her life.

I walked once again along the corridor of the last hospital where my mother received chemo. We were, as she wanted, closer to her home. The Specialist Tuberculosis and Lung Diseases Clinic in Koszalin. I'd push her down the halls in a wheelchair. We'd buy something sweet from the hospital cafeteria. We'd get lost. We laughed about it. And then I remembered. My mother loved life. She loved: squatting and peeing on the forest floor with her face tilted up, staring at the sun, smelling damp leaf cover, shaking dew from the leaves. We peed together. We closed our eyes together. Inhaled the herbs crushed in our hands. We took off our shoes and socks to press our feet into the moss. Together.

'Let's go to Mielno, Mum! You already had chemo today. It's fifteen minutes away. No one will notice.'

'No. I don't want to go to the seaside. Not now. I don't want to enjoy life anymore. I've stopped caring. I've said my goodbyes.'

She was in love with the sea. But she didn't want to die in the sea. And now she'd rejected it. And now she was dying.

Agony doesn't always end in death.

There are three stages of death: clinical, biological, and psychic. First, clinical death. Then the inter-mortal stage, then the brain transitions to the state of biological death. To begin, circulation and respiration cease irreversibly. In the next few minutes, the final death of the entire brain occurs (psychic death).

There are two types of death. A person dies of disease complications, and in these cases death occurs either in the course of a long-term illness and is preceded by evident agony (slow death), or the death of a seemingly healthy person occurs suddenly and is a shock to those around them (sudden death).

Her slow death surprised me.

As if she were too delicate, too sensitive for mortality.

When I enter her apartment, the room where my mother is dying, I hear 'Days We Don't Know' by Marek Grechuta. Everyone knows how it goes: 'Only those days that we don't know yet are important.' An inappropriate soundtrack for dying. Especially for a person who does not believe in an after-life. The classic black humour of Radio Pogoda – a station for retirees – which played Grechuta several times a day. My mother and I didn't have time to joke about it.

As my mother dies, I try to somehow summarise her life. Just as some take stock of their lives in their thirties and forties. Particularly obsessive people do this at the end of each year. I find photos from different periods of my mother's life and we look at them together. I show her the paintings she painted. There's so many. I could use 'Days We Know' about now. It would go something like this: 'Only the days that are behind us are important.'

This was when my mother was not yet dead. Dead but not yet passed on, not yet departed. Mothers don't depart. Not from daughters. Maybe they depart from their sons? From authors? Różewicz's mother departed. My mother has never departed from me. She just died. My mother died. Undead mothers are difficult. The dead ones aren't interested in being even a little bit easier.

As if I couldn't believe in my existence and had to push it to the brink every few years. Birth and death. Nothing else interested me. None of that 'living' nonsense.

The weariness of this dying is unbearable. Boring, boring, boring. She's dying of boredom. But she doesn't know that she can't die like that. From draughts, sure. No one has died from a bad smell, but many have died from a draught. It takes a bit too long. She dies all year. A year as even as a cleft.

In the last two weeks before her death, she allowed me to be with her. Just like that. All day, every day. She didn't get tired of my presence, but I had to be discreet. Only now: trust, lots of good things, peace of mind that she is dying where she wanted – in her own room, in her own bed. Purchased three months before. Dying on an anti-decubitus mattress in a reha-bilitation bed.

I prepared shrimp in white wine for her. I drank the cooking wine and sensed that these were her last days in this world. I didn't know anything about the other one. I told her about the surprisingly good coffee from the machine at the entrance to Tesco. And also about warm dresses from a Polish brand on sale in a store in Kołobrzeg. No, I don't remember what I said. But I remember how. Two adult women were talking. Even though I was changing my mother's nappy now and she was changing me thirty years earlier, in March 2017 we met for a moment without these dependencies. I was so happy talking to her like that. I knew well that these memories would not fade. That these are moments to which I will return many times.

My great, crazy, greedy love for my mother. One of those rare loves worth talking about at all.

'I love you, Mum.'

'But I don't love you.'

'That's not true, I don't know why you said that, but I know you love me very much.'

'You yes, but not myself.'

'You don't love yourself? I was sure you were saying you didn't love me.'

'I've never loved myself,' she says and cries like a baby. Wet, snotty.

These, my mother's last words. When she was already unconscious, for three days before her death, I tried to convince her to love herself. Love yourself, Mum. I listed why she should love herself, why I love her so much. As if you could convince someone to love. As if you loved someone *for* something.

There are stages of dying. You can read about them, prepare yourself somehow. For example, in the fourth stage, the functions of the respiratory system begin to shut down. Inhalation usually stops first. It takes a few moments longer to exhale. In the fifth phase, the remnants of consciousness fade. This stage takes three to five minutes. Hearing lasts the longest. Even in the interlethal stage, also called inter-mortal, words reach the dead.

Be careful what you say around the newly dead!

'Cancer' rhymes with 'dancer', and the disease turned her into a drunken sleepwalker, even though she didn't drink.

When I was feeding my mother yesterday, she grabbed my hand. When she brought my hand holding the spoon to her mouth, I thought she wanted to kiss it. Sometimes she did that, out of gratitude. But this time, my mother bit me. She thought I was something to eat. That's what she said. My daughter, sitting next to her, imitated her grandmother. I fed them in turns – a spoonful for my mother, a spoonful for my daughter. When I massage my mother's feet – numb, aching, icy – her granddaughter lies down next to me. She lies limp and cries, 'Mama, rub my feet,' and howls in mock pain.

But there are minutes.

Today is the 8th of March. Women's Day. While preparing shrimp in butter and wine sauce for my daughter and mother in her kitchen, once again I pour myself white wine into a green glass. I look out the dirty window. Used nappies lie on the windowsill outside. I look at my grandmother's apartment opposite. There's something I like about this view. Four generations. The feminine continuum. I'm taking over her kitchen. Although in our world there were other options: the mother did not have to die for her daughter to live.

Tomorrow I will argue again with my mother, with my daughter, with my stepfather. Fight for home medical care, for them to test my mother's blood. And then I'll worry about the results. I need to arrange for further treatment. Get some morphine if she starts hurting. Order a drip if she stops eating. Or I will give up and just love her, love my daughter, love myself. I'll decide tomorrow.

My mum is dying. Comatose for the past three days, eyes closed. She dies in a room of her own. Because she has one, her own room.

I'm holding her hand. Every few moments, I moisten her lips. I wash her festering eyes and dry her nose with damp gauze. I shift her position delicately to prevent bedsores. I massage her legs and arms. I place cold compresses on her forehead and under her armpits when she breaks out in fever. I straighten her blanket. I stick opioid patches beneath her collarbones. Just in case. The patches make your breathing shallow, but she has little of it left anyway. My mother's face is calm but her breath restless. Her agonising wailing echoes throughout the entire apartment, down the stairwell. Deep, quick, loud inhales. Deep, quick, loud exhales. My ears are ringing.

Sometimes I talk to my mother. I ask her to finally love herself. I try to give her courage, I assure her of my love. Just in case. I take turns singing to her and then stop smiling because we both know I'm not the best at singing. Sometimes I don't say anything. I'm always holding her hand and she's holding mine – or so it seems to me. We listen to a lot of good music together. And a little less of the sentimental songs: Czesław Niemen's 'Memories' and Ewa Demarczyk's 'Tomaszów'. I leave her room. Maybe she needs space to die? Maybe I've lingered like an uninvited guest and now there's no way to end this life, because she would prefer to be alone?

For the last six hours I haven't left her room, not even to use the bathroom. I'm sitting in the chair beside her bed. At times I look out the window because my mother never liked me to stare at her for too long. I don't know why I read her books that I haven't read since high school: *Steppenwolf* by Hermann Hesse and *Remember to Remember* by Henry Miller. Then we'd read them together; we liked them together.

We have moments of silence full of tenderness, kisses, stroking, and caressing. I don't know what I'm doing, I've never done it before, and my mother wolf is dying. The last hour of her life. It seemed to me that I was asleep, that I was dreaming that yellow fluid gushed from her mouth. I look at my watch: three in the morning. In reality, hot, sunny foam bubbles in the crack of her mouth, making her breathing even louder. Unbearable. I wipe her lips, chin, neck, arms, and hands. I gently remove excess secretions from her mouth with a moistened cloth. Alternately terrified and composed. I cover her face with a paper towel so she doesn't spill everywhere and gently wipe her lips with a damp cotton pad. Calm. Mum, too. Breathing slows. I know she's dying. I've never been so sure about anything in my life. I feel a kind of dead calm.

The last two or three breaths are so infrequent that they are a minute apart. One last deep exhale. When I look at my watch, it's three forty-five. Mum is still warm. I can no longer hear her heart, but I can still feel the pulse on her wrist for a long time. Until four o'clock, I sit like this, with her narrow and smooth wrist under my fingers. It is quiet.

'You can die,' I told her.

I read somewhere that during pregnancy, you have to mentally release the baby into the world at just the right moment. Otherwise, they'll be born after the due date. I was terribly afraid of this deadline. That my mother would die after her due date. That she would explode, rot, wake up, and cry like a child who doesn't want to die.

As a child, I constantly thought about my mother's death to avoid being surprised by it. That's how afraid of it I was. When I finally stopped thinking about it, that's when she died.

3

I washed. Plucked. Applied make-up. I patted thick concealer onto the darkening undereye circles. High coverage. I blended the foundation with my fingertips, where it sat unabsorbed on top of cold skin and closed pores. Vichy, available in drug stores, formulated for mature skin, which looked so young that day. Face contouring next. My mother knew the tricks, knew about Kim Kardashian, who'd taught millions of women around the world how to hollow their faces with bronzer. Thanks to my mother, I also learnt how to darken my cheeks, temple, and chin to look skinnier. A poorly contoured face would be a double portrait. If I dragged the bronzer brush down the centre of my face, it would look divided, sunken. You have to paint yourself and the dead according to the principles of chiaroscuro: everything that is darker seems smaller, what's bright appears larger. Although all that glitters is not gold, as she said.

I highlighted my mother's cheekbones, the tip of her nose, and the centre of her forehead – for a rejuvenating effect. As if the cult of youth had a hold over coffins, too. Contrary to the belief that it is better to die older. Better late than too early. I brushed highlighter across her collarbones. When your collarbones stick out, you look skinny. Add a bit of shimmer above the upper lip. Dusting the pearlescent powder here makes the lips appear fuller. We'd read articles together with tips like 'How to Make Your Cupid's Bow Pop'. Secretly, of course. I tried to paint her in such a way as to highlight her assets. Or hide her imperfections. I remember how we laughed together at these hypocrisies.

I watched my mother do her eyes many times. I remembered what I had seen when she 'painted herself beautiful' – that's what she called it. So I applied light shadow on the moving eyelid and a slightly darker colour in the crease. I pulled up the skin along her lash line so that I could briefly see her green iris, and then drew a brown line. I mascaraed her long and straight eyelashes. I gave up on using an eyelash curler. I added eyebrows where they were too sparse.

As I was applying lipstick to her cracked, full lips, I blurted out, 'You're looking younger than me, Mum.'

In fresh, light, girlish posthumous make-up, my mother looked young and thin, but still dead.

Since the deceased can still hear for several hours after death, I gingerly told my mother that maybe she really did wear too much make-up. When she was alive, I didn't have the courage to make jokes about that.

Basic principles of tanatocosmetology: the deceased should look as if she were only sleeping, not dead. To achieve this effect, it's most important to give the skin the correct colour.

When the illusion of my mother's immortality collapses, I am left with only optical trickery. Her face really *does* look slimmer with well-placed bronzer. I believe in this illusion even on the day of her death. But she'd wanted a closed casket. After all, we wear make-up for ourselves, she said, not for others.

Her death wasn't dry. This wasn't a coincidence.

Do you know what a child with tonsillitis smells like? She smelled like that.

'If you could only take one thing to a desert island, what would it be, Mum?'

'Tweezers,' she said, 'but not for the eyebrows, you'll understand after menopause.' She stroked her chin like a man with a day's growth of stubble.

When she died, I knew what to do. I pulled the tweezers from her make-up bag. I plucked my mother's eyebrows. Hair removal was surprisingly easy, and left no redness because the skin was at an optimal temperature. I stroked my mother's smooth face one last time. Left hand. In my right, I held the tweezers poised in case I found some little bastard on her chin, above her lip, on a mole below the lip line – prime spots for plucking. I sat on the edge of the bed and carefully pulled her hair from her face, strand by strand. Once, I even let out a stifled laugh. But I quickly fell silent. After all, my mother could still hear me. I caressed her head. The hairstyle wasn't a challenge. I really wanted to comb her hair, wanted to touch the slippery, straight, thin pixie cut. But after chemo and radio-therapy, only a chestnut hedgehog had managed to grow back. I ran my hand over it with pleasure. After cancer treatment, hair grows stronger, thicker, more manageable.

I liked inhaling the scent of the skin on her head as she lay next to me. I loved her scent.

At the time of her death, my mother was fifty-nine years old and her only illness was cancer. None of that typical high blood pressure, no diabetes. Even her cholesterol was normal.

So I asked myself: what should I bury her in?

This is a very delicate matter between mother and daughter. I knew I'd dress her in cobalt blue. We'd talked about it. Dark blue. Indigo. Although I preferred her in autumnal colours. Now it seems cruel of me, to have said that. My mother had to prepare clothes for her coffin. After all, she was a woman from beyond Bug River, from the eastern border. Each of us, at a certain age, hangs clothes in the closet in case of death. For as long as I can remember, my grandmother has been updating her coffin wardrobe. She has been readying herself for the grave for at least thirty years. In my house, once you're over fifty, you can start preparing for your own burial. So I knew that the funeral outfit had to be somewhere in my mum's closet. But how was I supposed to recognise it? My grandmother showed me her coffin outfit. A black pantsuit in a garment bag. The only items in plastic. Like a body bag for roadside accidents.

Mum's wardrobe was full of dark blue clothes. It has been her favourite colour in recent years. I started my search with a plan: I was looking for something elegant but unsuitable for walking around town. Recumbent elegance. An elegant and elegiac outfit. This is what I'm looking for. My mother left behind no clues. No note on a hanger labelled 'casket clothes'. But she had to have them. I found a navy blue pencil skirt. Was this it? Or maybe the result of some shopping mistake, a passing fancy, or trend from years ago? Maybe it was her worst purchase? Something she hid with remorse at the back of the closet? At that time, my mother wore flared skirts. A-line, flattering for her figure. What if that navy skirt was an outfit about which my mother would say, 'I would never in my life wear that!'

'And after life, Mum?'

'Especially not then.'

Maybe it wasn't like that after all. After all, in her best days, she wore pencil skirts. This could have been her first choice. These could have been her new, better days.

But even if I got it wrong with the posthumous skirt, at least I did better with the top. Three months before her death, I bought my mother a tunic with a deep V, which was supposed to lengthen her neck, swollen post-steroids, and a fitted blouse, which tricks the eye into slimming the torso. Shades of midnight sky, of course. In the year of cancer, I only bought her elegant pyjama sets and airy bathrobes, and, from oncology stores, turbans, which she never wore. I only gave her one dress, perfect for a coffin, three months before her death, as a Christmas present. I had to make sure:

'This? You're sure? All right. What do you think? OK. We don't have to talk about it anymore.'

Thoughts churn. Thoughts create anecdotes. We'll laugh about all this someday. When everything turns out to be a mistake. You never got sick. You didn't die. I just thought you did. I was only kidding. Although no one thought my joke was very funny.

I ironed and cried. Because I didn't know how to iron out the wrinkles in the pencil skirt as neatly as my mother did.

'Hand it over! I'll do it myself. I can't watch you suffer,' she said.

My mother had been dead for four hours when I began to choke on tears for the first time. I tried to clear my throat of the pain in my chest. But it didn't want to break away. I ironed my clothes to no avail. I turned on the steam in the iron, turned it off, switched between temperatures and functions: cotton, wool, linen. Unable to figure it out.

How best to iron clothes for your mother's body? Thousands of women and men ask themselves this question every day, though it appears to be a very simple task. Fast, crease-free ironing is the dream of many orphans and, contrary to appearances, an easy one to fulfil. Get friendly with the iron after your mother's death.

Accessories, too. No easy task. I chose a long necklace with a blue orb encircled by a silver ring. It looked like Saturn on a chain. It elongated the silhouette. One ring, a thick silver band. A bracelet with blue stones: jasper, turquoise, agate, and ulexite. Although I associated my mother with lapis lazuli. I thought she asked me for this wrist ornament as part of readying herself for the grave. Because earlier, when she wasn't dying, she said that this bracelet I'd bought online reeked of cheapness. I gave in to her on a whim, which in the face of death must have had some other, deeper meaning. Or not.

Even if it was just a dying whim, it felt good to fulfil. Because accessories are of utmost importance.

Shoes, then. Yes or no? We didn't have time to go over them. But since she was so fond of slippers when she was alive, I had to choose one. She had several dozen pairs. All clean and well kept. As I looked through her shoe closet, I cried over new boots, new heel tips, unopened pairs of tights. She'd had to throw away all her high heels. She didn't wear them anymore, and our feet were different sizes. I couldn't put on my dead mother's shoes. I decided to bury her in navy blue loafers, the taller ones, with a four-centimetre square heel. She hadn't had the time to break them in.

The temperature of her dead body, though low, wasn't yet icy, allowed for hugging, for warming your daughterly body with the maternal one.

I clung to her enough to last me a long time. I put her on an anti-bedsore mattress and lay next to her. Even when she died. I didn't tell anyone. It was our secret. I snuggled under her arm, even though she was already dead. Just like there is attachment parenting, I practised daughterly attachment. Skin to skin contact. After birth, the first two hours are crucial to building a bond between mother and baby. These minimums probably exist after death, though there's no research on the topic. Just to be on the safe side, I hugged her for two hours. I wanted closeness with her after death. Good thing I was running out of breast milk at the time. Otherwise, like Pero breastfeeding her condemned father, I might have tried to latch her. And so I just lay close to her. It didn't last long.

I waited until eight o'clock to make the official phone call.

'Doctor, my mother died at three forty-five in the morning. Can you come and confirm the death?' I asked – that was part of the family doctor's duties. But I said it without the contrition in my voice I had been practising over the last year in the presence of oncologists.

'I'll just reschedule my morning appointments and then I'm on my way,' he replied neutrally.

He arrived at a quarter past eight. He looked at her as if he found her attractive. No muss, no fuss.

The Prussian blue nail polish had not yet dried on my mother's hands when the men from the funeral home arrived to collect her body.

'Can you gentlemen wait a moment? I just painted my mum's nails,' I said to the two men from the Hades, Cerberus, or maybe Hourglass Funeral Home, pointing to my mother's near-perfect manicure. Her almond nails looked like acrylics.

It got awkward. They waited a few seconds, before, just after nine o'clock, they put the body in a bag and placed it on a stretcher. Quickly, in silence. And it wasn't a quick-drying polish: *sixty seconds*.

Then more things I didn't know.

'What about the nappy? My mum was wearing it at the end. But I guess I can take it off now?' I asked funeral experts.

'No, it has to stay on. Stuff often leaks out and things need to be washed or, worst case, changed.'

'I didn't know, but I guess if it has to,' I replied, wondering whether my mother would be mad at me for burying her in a nappy.

'We put most of the dead in coffins wearing nappies. Oh, and do you still have any burp cloths? It's worth covering her mouth with it for now. In case something leaks out. We don't want to get blamed for any stains.'

I quickly took my mother's silk scarf from the drawer, matching the colour to her outfit, and wrapped it around her face. It smelled strongly of her perfume. Her signature scent.

Expensive. Despite being a mid-range fragrance: Comme une Evidence by Yves Rocher, which I bought for her regularly.

'Shame to use such a nice scarf, no? You'll probably have to throw it away,' the undertaker assured me.

'Oh well. She won't lie with a burp cloth on like a child. She's a grown woman.'

My mother died because she couldn't breathe, because she couldn't inhale, because she had nothing to inhale.

My mother died three days before my thirty-second birthday. Three days earlier, on the 13th of March, she stopped speaking. I didn't like the way she walked around the apartment, muttering to herself. She'd wake at four in the morning. Always at the same time. For as long as I can remember, she considered this the waking hour prompted by her internal clock. I would check this myself, when I came back from the eighth-grade dance and other first-time parties at four in the morning, seeing if my mum was already awake. She would sit on a stool in the kitchen by the window. With strong black coffee. Did she take it with sugar? I don't remember now. I've already forgotten. So it's begun: my mother is disappearing. At least I remember that her favourite coffee is a few flat teaspoons of Arabica with boiling water. Sipped from brown Duralex.

I was convinced that it would always be like this: my mother was always supposed to drink coffee from this glass. Duralex was never supposed to break. I must have already sensed something when, after many attempts to throw the glass against the tiles, the impact-resistant mug finally shattered. Strangely. Into pieces fine as poppy seed. My mother must have been made of Duralex, too.

She died at the same time she woke up, four at night, four in the morning, the hour of death. The time when people with depression wake. Human babies are most often born at this hour. And when human mothers most often die. I don't know what's typical outside of the human species. I should check.

In her own room: she didn't rattle through the terminal phase –
that wouldn't have been right. She lived through it, then she
died, and what could be worse?

My mother died in a room overlooking a Tesco. In the room next to her kitchen, with the same view where she drank pour-over Arabica, smoked Karos, and stared into the middle distance. There used to be a patch of greenery sticking out from behind the apartment blocks. She fixed her gaze there. There was lots to look at. But they quickly built another superstore in this place. My mother remained loyal to Intermarché, Biedronka, and Netto. These were her supermarkets. In short: Tesco didn't last long.

Waiting and waiting, she manoeuvred the blinds so that she could see everything but others wouldn't be able to see her. In her own room, she looked through green blinds, and in the kitchen through red blinds. In her own room, she placed a round white table with a green openwork tablecloth and two white curved Thonet chairs. She hung her paintings and botanical engravings in frames on the walls. She painted the wooden built-in wardrobe mint green. On the smaller, white one, she placed photos of me, and flowers in a glass vase. From potted plants: lavender. From outside: wildflowers. Depending on the season, fresh or dried. There was also a small, chunky old TV set there. And in the middle: the bed on which she dozed at noon, lay and thought in the afternoon, slept and gnashed her teeth at night. I never saw her disturb the order of the books in the wicker basket next to the bed.

It was different in the kitchen. Yellowed plaster flaked off the ceiling. The '70s kitchen cabinets fell apart when yanked open. Gas stove. Table and stool. Scratched walls. Everything the colour of bruised flesh. She liked spending her days there. She liked kitchens. She liked to look out the window as people walked between the blocks.

I still think about it all.

They say mothers are always dead, just as children are always alive.

Just as we talk about 'home births', we could talk about 'home deaths'. I didn't get to give birth at home, but my mother managed to die at home. Natural childbirth. Natural death. If the dead talked about their deaths this way, my mother could boast that she died a natural death at home. A hippie among the dead. Eco-dead.

'And where did you die?'

'At home.'

'Wow, really? That's great,' the envious other dead person replies insincerely. 'Weren't you afraid?'

'No, I had a doula, a professional companion, my daughter.'

'I wanted to have a home death, too, but there were complications. I'm happy with how it turned out. Otherwise who knows if I would have died at all.'

'Oh, sure. The most important thing is that it worked. Doesn't matter where. The important thing is that the death's healthy.' False modesty with a dash of superiority.

'And they say that after a cesarean death (because they finally took me to the operating room and I died on the operating table), it's impossible to breastfeed.'

'I heard that, too. That's why I wanted to die at home. So, are you breastfeeding?'

'Yes. The most important thing is that death be brought to your breast quickly. Those first minutes are crucial.'

'Well, it's great that you're feeding naturally after death. Despite the, you know, cesarean and all. They say that a formula-fed soul is more sickly, more prone to obesity.'

'Right, I've read that. But let me tell you, I don't see any difference. My friend died at home like you, and her soul is still sick and she breastfed for only two months after she died.'

Mother!
Afterwards, no strength remains.
Her body's got flabby.
Why?
She tears the blood out from her veins
She does it for her baby.

I was supposed to burn you, I know that. Cremate you. You were afraid of waking up in a coffin, mouth full of wood, larva in your eyes. I know, I was supposed to do this after you died, Mum. But somehow I didn't feel I should.

There was no priest at my mother's funeral. She'd begged me: 'Promise me? No priest. And no hourglasses.' I promised her and did as she asked. The funeral home at the municipal cemetery proposed hiring a 'master of ceremonies' instead.

'We don't have one of our own. But you can hire a master from a big city. The closest one lives in Poznań, but his schedule is full. Next week should work though.'

The person conducting the funeral calls the family members himself, collects information about the deceased, and prepares a professional eulogy. He directs the entire ceremony. After all, he is the master.

Some strange man was supposed to speak over my feminist mother's corpse? Over my dead body! That's when I decided to become an occasional mistress of ceremonies.

'You can prepare thirty minutes of music on a flash drive. It will be played in the chapel, and then you can even say something into the microphone, and the gentlemen will come in and get the coffin, and the procession will follow the gentlemen, who will put the coffin in the ground. There will be a scoop in case someone wants to pour some dirt onto the coffin. And that's it,' the owner of the funeral home explained to me. It was actually Athena.

I made a playlist of music that my mother really liked. But without going overboard, no musical guilty pleasures. Except for one song – 'Mama' by Vitas. She loved this boy who sang about his mother's death. When she played the song for me for the first time, we cried together. Just like with Bob Marley and Buena Vista Social Club – a mother's teary compilation. My choice for her funeral.

We listened to the popular music for half an hour. I let it run through the last song and got distracted. I was late with my eulogy. But no one noticed anything. There were fifteen, maybe twenty people. They found out about the funeral through word of mouth.

Is the perfect funeral a perfect crime?

Really, I could have taken the microphone and said something nice, that my mother was a good woman, and that it was tragic to have died so young, but no one knows when they'll die, life is unexplored, and life after death even less so, though perhaps eternity exists, or maybe not, but in either case there's no need to fret, it's better to remember to keep remembering, or something like that.

But writing a eulogy takes many years. When you finally stand before your mother's coffin with all the words you've accumulated over this time, you may decide to wait for the gift of improvisation. Still, I didn't dramatically drop my pages of notes. I wasn't speaking off the top of my head. I read what I had scribbled moments earlier. I wrote the eulogy in a café – how pretentious, just as I preferred. It could have been an impressive, provocative, and witty performance, like in an American movie. But it was sentimental, modest, tactful, full of literary references, like in Polish films, especially those by Smarzowski. An ungrateful text littered with clumsy sentences. That's how sentences arrange themselves after a mother's death. As if every thought might find its way to her. I read the speech: hewn, solid, and solemn. Although I could never really afford to be reverent with myself. It's different with my mother. Sometimes I was overly pathetic. And my mother didn't like pathos or forcing someone to say something nice.

This was probably the first time I destroyed a deeply painful loss with cliché.

March deaths all have something in common.

'March is sullen and it's glum, it does in old men and the dumb.'

We walked behind the coffin in silence. It was raining. Although there was no indication of it before. When we entered the chapel, the sun had been shining. 'When a good man dies, it always rains,' my mother liked to say. Something about angels crying in heaven.

I was so happy about the rain that I sang her favourite dirge. But to be consistent with the secular funeral ceremony, it sounded like this: 'Noble hedgehog, lord of hosts, grant unto her eternal rest.' Again, with more and more vibrato in the voice that always made us laugh: 'Nooo-ble hedge-hoooog…' And then – I read this on my phone just before the funeral and translated it in a secular way:

'Let eternal light shine upon her, where all the dreamers reign.'

Nobody seemed to notice. Several people sang with me. That took courage.

When your mother dies, it feels like the insides – those in your chest – are being ripped out with bare hands, and yet it's a little worse than that.

My stepfather. He wanted to bury his wife in the family plot, above his mother. Himself, he wanted over his sister.

And so it was.

My mother was buried above her third mother-in-law. The day after my thirty-second birthday. I thought I wouldn't survive it.

My mum's brother died. My mother died. Meanwhile, our children feel these deaths. The kind of deaths that reek of vodka. From mouths, from clothes, especially denim jackets and leather jackets, scarves, hair.

I know I'm not crying over the fact that my mother didn't live to tell me her biography. I'm crying because *I* didn't live to see her tell me about it.

'When you're fifty, we'll sit down and have an honest talk,' she assured me.

It seems to me that this caesura shifted over the years. She once said we'd talk when I turned thirty. Then she said that was too early. In *The Lost Daughter*, Elena Ferrante writes about the age of fifty – only at this age is a daughter ready to hear her mother's story. Mother as a person, not just a function. That's what my mother thought, too.

I was your daughter, so I invented you as my mother. You were my invention.

I wanted to die with you so badly then, Mum.

How would a headline read? What would the tabloids write about my mother's death and my period of sadness?

Unbelievable But True! Perfectly Healthy Woman Falls Victim to Deadly Cancer!

Daughter Exposes Scandalous Truth Behind Mother's Mysterious Death! The Inside Story!

Humiliating Twist! Woman Succumbs to Illness Without Any Symptoms!

Daughter's Bizarre Life After Mother's Death Exposed! Shocking Details Inside!

Tragic Mystery: How Did This Young, Vibrant Woman Meet Her Untimely End?

Revealed: The Surprising Type of Mothers Who Die Young! Are You at Risk?

Grieving Your Mum? These Surprising Diet Secrets Promise Quick Recovery from Sorrow!

Daughter's Agony: A Sudden Epidemic of Mothers Dying! What's Going On?

Funeral Fashion Fiasco! You Won't Believe How They Dressed Her – The Shocking Back View!

With each death, I become worse.

Confession – a critical component of therapeutic action.

The confessor risks repercussions with every disclosure.

Confession demands that we listen and makes of us hostages to the truth.

Confession is no longer an act of truth, but rather a narcissistic spectacle.

Speaking ill of your mother is always a confession that bears a heavy price for us daughters.

My mum is dead. This is a confession.

4

My mother is in the ground. Since she died, I have had an ambivalent relationship with sand, gravel, dirt, pavements, and even floors. I know I'd feel better if I walked on the ground. If I could stand firm. If I could take root. But I'm afraid I'll touch her. She's in the ground. I'm on the ground. We have no shared space. One of us would need to break through. I lie down on the black earth where I buried her. She pokes out the other side. We connect, embrace. We have only the earth. And sand in our eyes. Clumps of black dirt. I'm desperate to lie on the ground, face down, with my belly towards my mother. I'd trickle down to her. Salty. Lonely. Uprooted.

When will I finally start thinking those now unthinkable thoughts?

Unless someone close to us dies, we think we'd like to lose weight. We continue to dream of slim mothers. Pray that the weight gain after pregnancy, after children, menopause, after forty does not burden us through fate or genetics. 'When I'm grown up and skinny,' we think. 'When I'm taller and have lost weight.' The first time my mother gained weight, I was eight and she was thirty-five. I told the other kids in the court-yard my mum was pregnant and I would have younger siblings. I didn't want a new sister or brother. But even more than that, I didn't want anyone to think my mum was fat. So when my mother called me a month before her fall and subsequent cancer diagnosis to tell me that she had lost a lot of weight, I remember being happy. Even though she was worried that she weighed five or seven kilograms less than a month before.

'But you wanted to lose weight,' I reassured her calmly.

'Well, yes, but it happened so fast, and without dieting,' she continued, and I thought she was craving my attention in a strange way. If I'd been able to overcome this obsession with a slim figure, I might have noticed earlier that she was dying. Maybe not.

I remember that at the oncology ward, before they discovered her cancer, my mother told the doctor that she had lost weight and that it worried her. To which the oncologist replied with surgical precision that losing three to five kilograms a month is good, but anything beyond that should scare us.

My mother has been dead for two years, and this is the first time I've thought of this conversation. I didn't listen to her premonitions, I couldn't believe that losing a few kilos was dangerous. I didn't want to think about it. I wasn't thinking.

My mother's death casts a stark light on my life, but my senses remain dull. It's a lie that what doesn't kill you makes you stronger. I have never felt as weak as I do now.

On the 'Beekeeping Discussion Form Under the Auspices of the Michalow Apiary', in the section 'The home for real bee enthusiasts', I found a thread entitled: 'No mother. What now?' No, I didn't enter this question into the search engine. Or maybe I did? If I'm being honest, yes, I could have done it. I expected to see 'No results'. Instead, as I followed subsequent conversations between beekeepers about the hives in which the queen had died, I despaired. In beekeeping jargon, there is even a word for a honeybee colony without a queen: 'queenless'. Experts write that 'queenlessness can only be inferred from the bees' behaviour and the sounds from the hive. The bees howl loudly and lift their abdomens high.'

Mourning turned me into a reader of beekeeping forums, eavesdropping on hives with dead mothers. In Chomiczówka, on Rodziny Połanieckich Street, there are two apiaries and a stretch of meadow, soon be destroyed by the planned S7 motorway. It was there that I first heard the distinctive sounds of the queenless.

An extended mourning period is sure to follow.

kardek writes:

Hello, fellow beekeepers.

I have a problem: my bees swarm out of the hive when it gets below −18. In November, I noticed symptoms of queenlessness in this colony. It was a healthy and strong colony, well fed and treated against varroa. I last checked on them on the 15th of September. Around the beginning of November, I noticed signs of queenlessness. The characteristic humming sound and bees running around the hive walls. I looked inside and couldn't find the queen. I would like to emphasise that I did not harm the queen because I hadn't opened the hive since the 15th of September, and after opening it in November there was still some capped brood, so the mother must have been there after the 15th. I didn't have a spare queen or a way to combine the colonies, so on the advice of a beekeeper friend, I left them as they were. Now I've I noticed several dozen (20–30) dead bees in the snow outside the hive. They break out at frosts of −18 (today I saw one leave, fly about two metres, and freeze up). I found several traces of brown spots next to the bees – droppings.

What could have happened to the mother? Why are the bees exiting the hive? Is there hope for the colony's survival? Is there anything I can do to help them? And if they survive and there is really no mother there, what should I do with the queenless in the spring?

Regards.

Queenless after winter – 3130 views.

oldschool writes:

At this point, there's not much you can do. There's only one way to make sure they don't suffer. Tip the hive onto the snow. In these temperatures, it'll be a quick end.

kardek writes:

Thanks for the response. So, the behaviours I've observed indicate the end of the colony? I should mention that the bees from this hive were exceptionally active compared to the others before the frost. They roamed around the entrance and flew about when the others were quiet. Is this another sign of queenlessness?

oldschool writes:

Yes, these are the exact signs of trouble in the colony or that the mother is gone.

Bees without a queen behave completely differently. You can see their nervousness. They walk quickly, go out, go in, go out, go in. They enter the hive, fly away, and then quickly return. There's an audible hum near the hive, buzzing. Now you'll know better in the future. Best of luck.

PS It's always better to merge queenless families, otherwise they won't survive the winter!

kardek writes:

OK. I'm not doing anything because there's nothing I can do anyway.

I'll wait until spring.

Oh, and if anyone has an overwintered queen available for sale, I'd be grateful :)

The post has received 0 likes.

A stranger tells me that she has just been diagnosed with lung cancer. And then we go dancing in Reverb. Five of us. We dance in a circle, or rather in a pentagram. It's too dark. Cheap, stinking smoke rises. The girl with cancer dances opposite me. Dressed in black, she increasingly resembles a shadow, an outline of a figure, death. Her movements remind me of my own. In dance therapy, we talk about the reflection of movement. *Mirroring*. Treatment technique: the therapist tries to imitate the patient's movement. It's about passing another person's traffic through yourself. I let her through. I don't know who is whose mirror image. I am dancing with lung cancer, with my mother's cancer, a cancer that I fear every day. The day before, I had a lung CT scan. I got the results. Fast, through an acquaintance. I didn't hear: 'Did anyone come with you to the appointment?', as they say to those with a diagnosis. I am calm. Although not entirely, because it was not a precise tomography, one with contrast. I am allergic to contrast.

In the same hospital, two weeks earlier, a girl with cancer was asked about her support network. She'd received a prognosis. In the same hospital doctors deal with delivering so-called bad news by adopting a humorous attitude. They like jokes in the style of 'A woman walks into the doctor's office and the doctor says':

'Could you tell me your Zodiac sign?'

'I'm a Capricorn,' she replies.

The doctor nods thoughtfully. 'Well, according to my chart, you have cancer.'

I know because my husband works there.

I imagined not having a mother would be different.

I can't breathe, Mum.

I'm scared.

Where are you now, Mum?

Mum, where did you go?

You'll never hug me again?

You'll never argue with me again?

Will you ever speak to me again?

To be honest, I died a little too, Mum.

Do you still worry about me?

I can't breathe.

And it hurts a lot under my breasts.

For two years now.

It's like a long mourning stroke.

I think some mints fell down the wrong pipe.

The Ice Fresh fell into my heart, Mum.

It hurts like I'm dying, and then a little worse.

I read that a healthy mourning period lasts a year.

The longer I don't see you, the more I miss you.

You're still not back, Mum.

How long should I wait?

Our love was beautiful and unhealthy.

She looked so beautiful in my dream today. I stroked her smooth face. She came back to life. Dreams give me the greatest happiness. I'm in bliss when I look at her. I find myself falling in love with my own mother. All over again. In this dream, I was happy but she looked uncomfortable. 'If I knew you loved me so much, I wouldn't have hidden myself. I wouldn't have played dead for the last two years,' she said. I didn't resent her. I embraced her and cried with happiness. There was no joy without her.

In my dreams my mother is always alive and dressed in indigo. She simply moved to Mexico. Sometimes she threatened me with the possibility of moving somewhere far away, dying her hair blonde, so no one would find her. If I hadn't been with her until the end, pronounced her dead myself, and then fixed her make-up in the casket, I might have clung to the hope that she had done just that: not died, but lived on as a blonde in Mexico. There, she would have her yellow and cornflower blue kitchen. The colours she used in her paintings would finally see the right light.

It doesn't matter how much I dream about her. She's still dead.

Between the ages of two and five, children learn the concept of death but don't comprehend that it's irreversible. When a mother dies, we regress to this state. Death reverses in dreams, in slips of the tongue, in the gestures of strangers. She's come back. She'll come back.

All mourners dream of the reanimated dead. And I dream about my mother nearly every night. In my dreams she poses for my book. The way she maybe wanted to be described. Attractive, cordial, fragrant, laughing, eloquent, smooth, unattainable. That's how I remember her – unattainable. No one could have her. She slipped out of the monikers of wife and lover with men, and I couldn't have her as a mum.

Who would have thought that my mother would break my heart?

But each morning you have to face the fact that she is indeed
dead.

I want nothing more than to wake up, make myself a cup of coffee, and call her. Hear her answer in a good mood and say in that raspy, sensual voice of hers:

'Good morning, Niteczko!'

That's how she appeared in my dream last night.

'Maman died today. Or maybe yesterday, I can't be sure' – this is how Camus's *The Stranger* begins. Thanks to *The Stranger*, I fell in love with literature. I shared this fascination with my mother. This was when I would put my experiences into words that I would use to convey each one to her. This was when I was talking to her in my mind all the time. But I never, ever wanted to start a book as brilliantly as Camus. Or did I? Now, writing about her on weekdays, I naïvely believe that this will somehow save her from oblivion, but will also help me rebuild myself, achieve independence. A new identity. Matricidal maniac. Someone who uses her mother's death as a source of meaning-making for her days. As long as my mother lived, I was a daughter. But when she died, I lost this identity: I won't ever be anyone's daughter again. And that's the only thing I was really good at: daughterhood. A part of me has fallen away. Her death killed the daughter in me. Or I killed her.

I was a grateful daughter. If this is true, why do I question my conscience so often?

I imagined all these terrible things about mothers and daughters. What kind of mother will I be when I die? One that is difficult to think back on? These are the bonds that colour our entire lives. She wanted me to write. I did everything she wanted. Now I'll write this and finally feel relief.

Where's my relief?

I was the daughter of a single mother. This is what I built my identity on. This was my starring role. That it was a supporting role – oh well. At least it was steady work, or so I thought. I was a mother's daughter. And that's why this loss of identity hurts so much. That this is a chance to see myself as someone else, someone more than a daughter? I doubt it. I'm less than that.

I read that the earlier a mother dies, the worse it is for the child. The more abrupt, the harder it is to come to terms with. They've done studies. No, not experimental ones. No one's killing mothers in the name of science. These studies show that daughters whose mothers died suddenly, for example in a plane crash, are more likely to be stuck in mourning. Most likely it's because they didn't have the opportunity to say goodbye, unlike in the case of cancer or another creature that slowly steals mothers away from well-behaved children. And yet I was stuck, liminal. Limping.

Motherless daughters have already gone to bed, each beside their dogs, cats, husbands, wives, or children. They all sleep in the same way.

'What do you have a problem with?'

'Death.'

For people with a mortality problem. For those who can't stop thinking about death, other people's and their own – I propose Mortals Anonymous. Using a twelve-step programme, you will achieve complete abstinence: no thoughts of death. There are those among us who have not thought about death for a year, three years, and some even for a decade. We believe that it is impossible to indulge in even the smallest memory of a deceased person. Every such thought is a trap. Our offer also includes a proposal for ACAM – Adult Children of Anonymous Mortals. Because the fact that you were once addicted to the thought of death has a profound impact on your children. Join us.

Mortals Anonymous is a community of men and women sharing their experiences, strength, and hopes to aid personal and collective recovery from the obsession with mortality. Participation is open to anyone with a genuine desire to stop dwelling on thoughts of deceased loved ones. There are no mandatory fees in MA; we are self-supported and operate through voluntary contributions. MA is unaffiliated with any sect, denomination, political group, organisation, or institution, abstains from public debates, does not support or oppose any views. Our primary purpose is to remain thoughtless about the dead and to support other mortals in achieving the same.

My psychotherapist friends ask me if my mother's death was liberating. It wasn't. There was no relief. No new-found motivation. However, in the aftermath of her death, I did a lot of stupid things. I seduced a nineteen-year-old. I drank, manipulated, got doped up. Maybe it was for the best. Without being clichéd: I came back to life and savoured it. The genuine joy I found in small things had died. It's dead to me. It was in her. Just like a cancerous tumour, which I dreamed was inside me. But the metastases were in her.

After her death, she's in me all the more. I am closer to her now than ever before. What relief can there be in this? What did you think? What notions do you harbour about life after your mother's death? The love only intensifies. I've chosen to live with my dead mother, to celebrate my dreams with her, even if they tear me from everyday life.

My mother finds ways to break through. To me. She visits me many times. Since she died, every thought is a trap. A flashback. I know this one from hallucinogenic mushrooms and my mother. My psychedelics, both natural, incapacitating. Things I might do after my mother's death: survive the loss, not lose my mother, avoid becoming her.

After a betrayal, you can't watch movies with betrayal plots. Not even TV shows. Is it safe to watch films about dying maternal figures after a mother's death? Or at least read books with mother-deaths?

'My precious daughter, do you know why there are no books about women my age in all this classic literature?' my mother asked me.

'Because when it was being written, women your age were long dead, Mum,' I answered quickly.

Amused, my mother repeated this anecdote from my childhood on many occasions. I didn't like this story. I'm only starting to find it funny now.

Mother!
    Afterwards, no strength remains.
    Her body's got flabby.
    Why?
    She tears the blood out from her veins
    She does it for her baby.

I thought this was my responsibility: to nurture this guilt. For my mother's death, for her unfulfilment and loneliness.

I'm crazy about you, Mum. As I write this, it's already late. You died last spring. March, the 16th of March. A perverse date, the intended date of my birth – and that of my daughter. Neither of us – me or your granddaughter – arrived on that date to start our lives. You succeeded with your end. You doubled it on the 16th of March by starting to die and dying. On the 16th of March 2016, a fall led to the discovery of your cancer. It settled in your kidneys, brain, lungs, and lymph nodes. It could have been lurking since New Year's Eve. Small cell, metastatic, a malignant crab in the lungs.

After her death, I was faced with a choice: to radically change or not. I chose the latter, thereby acknowledging my life as it was before the year of the cancer.

That's everything. This was my new life without her. It was the ultimate sadness. Yet, I knew that life could still fuck with me. I had a feeling that as long as my mother was alive, my youth would last, and that after her death, reality would descend upon me, in some completely surreal way. A counterfeit feeling of life. The last throes of youth, as they say, arrive when your mother dies, but she's not dead yet. A period associated with carefreeness, with a belief that everything would work out, the feeling that the world is open and infinite, that death doesn't exist. But death has already occurred. However, it never completely obliterated everything. Previous deaths chipped away at me piece by piece. They even bestowed a certain nobility to my youth. But never to this extent. This 'so much' was never supposed to exist.

And to think I used to care so much.

The most common reactions to a mother's death are apathy, addiction to psychoactive substances, and promiscuity.

How long after the death of a loved one should you abstain from sex? I know the recommendation after giving birth (six weeks). After a cesarean section (six weeks). If the cervix shortens during pregnancy (until childbirth). But how long after the death of a loved one, so as not to traumatise yourself with mourning sex? I don't know. Maybe six weeks too? Self-help books for mourners provide no handy rubrics. Just recommendations not to get pregnant too quickly. Why? After giving birth, it's clear: the body needs time to heal. But after the death of a loved one, you should probably wait to get pregnant, so as not to replace the deceased person with a newborn. Not to be like the people who buy a puppy immediately after the death of their beloved dog. There's something dishonest about it. It's difficult to trust their love.

Something's happened. Within myself, in you, and in those on other continents. But nobody has heard anything about it.

Motherless women appear older than they are. No one asks: 'Did you have a facelift or did your mother pass away?' They're more likely to think: 'Either her mother is dead or she's been neglecting herself.' When my mother died, I was nearing thirty-three. But prematurely joined the ranks of an older group, whose mothers died when their daughters were closer to fifty. I wanted to stay young and energetic, to keep this death invisible on me. So that there would be no trace of the year I spent taking care of my dying mother. I wanted someone to say: 'Wow, and you've also been coping with your mother's death. It doesn't show at all, you're holding up so well.' But, of course, no one says that. Meanwhile, the daughters of non-dead mothers have smoother, more radiant skin.

To the current owners of mothers:

Don't flaunt them with impunity. Do it in secret. I was once in possession of a mother you'd die for. Everyone wanted one like mine. This made me special. Like mother, like daughter.

Women talking with their mothers on the phone have become unbearable.

I know I won't go grocery shopping with my mum. Or any other kind of shopping. That was in another life. That was in life.

When I'm alone in the kitchen, I whisper, 'Mum.' I know I will never say 'Mum' to anyone again.

The kitchen is a lonely place.

It was an entire year after her death before I found a note taped inside a kitchen cabinet door.

'Pickled cucumbers: 4 flat tablespoons of salt per 3 litres of water.'

Her handwriting. Her place. Her kitchen. My tears. My no-place. My loss.

'I've got a good track record with cancers.' I hear this fragment of a conversation between two women at a café table beside mine.

Of course, they mean men, astrological Cancers. But I immediately think of oncology. About someone saying about me: 'She's got a good track record with cancers. Her mum died of a malignant lung tumour.'

And then I have to calm myself down. It's not like anyone says things like that.

I never had a backup plan that included finding a replacement for my mother.

I'm thirty-three years old. I think about the smells of various plants and soils. I remember the ice cream flavors from my childhood, the pleasure of walking alone down the streets of large cities, purseless, my hands in my pockets.

'I died and you're still so preoccupied with your own happiness?'

No, my mother would never say that to me.

I thought about those who, like me, had lost themselves at thirty-three. About Jesus, who took his own life then. It's not an easy age.

Please let me be sad a little longer.

How should you cope with the death of your mother? Maternal death is not contagious. You can be friends with an orphan, and your mother will still live for a long time. Maternal death is not contagious. You can be friends with an orphan, and your mother will still live for a long time. Maternal death is not contagious. Only sad.

A few months after my mother's death, when I was looking through her small collection of books, I found a note in her handwriting beneath my dedication to her: 'This is a lie, like everything else you say.' I started shaking. Then I cried for a long time. The dedication was sincere and simple: 'For the best mum, whom I love and admire.' I wasn't lying, not this time.

Having such a difficult mother is the best thing that ever happened to me. That she was in my life for over thirty years. Sometimes remembering this is enough to make me happy. For that, I'm grateful.

There is nothing unique about a mother's death. Almost everyone will experience one. Mothers should die before their children, that's the order of things. I trade in on the fact that my mother died when I was of reproductive age. When I was giving birth to children, my mother died. Usually mothers die later, mine wasn't even sixty. It's fucking depressing. If I included her death in my experiences, maybe I would start living. Or maybe I would never forgive myself for trying to gain something from her death.

mothers – sad women
mothers after therapy – feral women
mothers reconciled – fat women
mothers without mothers – empty women

I'm afraid that I'll take even her death from her. Even this. Even after I've already stolen so much of her time and opportunities. Not to mention the prenatal period when – as everyone always says – daughters steal their mother's beauty, while sons enhance it.

i killed or injured my own mother, killed or injured, many times i've injured her, i did not kill my mother

When did my mother become death itself?

she's not here she's not here she's not here she's not here she's not here she's not here she's not here

I keep telling myself to stop waiting and start living – although there is probably no such thing as 'starting to live'. But I remember that I was once alive. Before she died.

Even if we don't suffer from high blood pressure, obesity, or old age, the mantra 'she's not here' can lead to a heart attack. It hurts so much. My left hand goes numb. I'm choked with pain. I start coughing because doctors say you should cough when you're having a heart attack. So I cry and cough. Even though I don't feel like coughing at all. But I wanted to cry so much. If only I could cry without these pre-infarction symptoms. I really have to change the subject.

Every minute, tons of mothers die and people handle this effortlessly, without making a big fuss. Some even take advantage of the situation. They learn a lesson. Or maybe they're just fooling us. Because somehow I can't do the same.

I have to do a lot of things instead of her now:

    modulate my voice to sound firm;

    greet saleswomen as if we were friends;

    exude warmth;

    shine my shoes, because they reveal your character;

    get up at four in the morning and drink coffee, because no one else will do it for me;

    manage everything myself;

    fly away while creating, except I don't paint, I'm a different kind;

    carry grocery bags;

    sing to children when they wake in the morning:

Who's awake? Who's awake? All children ask.

    Who's awake? Who's awake? (Insert child's name here)! And now the sun can shine.

and for goodnight:

    Lullaby, lullaby (insert child's name here), lullaby, lullaby (insert child's name here), my little daughter, lullaby, lullaby (insert child's name here).

I still have so much to do.

I only came to understand my mother's immortality after her death. How the hell was I supposed to know? That there would be more of my mother now and that she'll never really die. How was I supposed to know that?

I am struck by the slowness: it's been two years since my mother died, and the mourning is only just beginning. My mother's absence is only beginning to reveal itself. It is clear that I still have a long way to go through this painful absence. And that it will touch me at different times and in different positions. I am surprised by new places where I experience these whiplashes. This suffering escalates. Meanwhile, everything converges in absence (sadness, anger, fear) and complex emotions (longing, love, disbelief).

Without a shadow of hope that these stories about my mother will reveal any meaning, I can tell them until the very end, because I can, because I can afford it, because only such a life seems fair to the deceased.

There's something else. The tongue. It can't keep up with her absence. It freezes in my mouth. Sticking to the backs of slippery teeth, it crests at the palate and falls into a warm, moist, safe recess. It does not tear the ligament. It transforms my loss into someone else's. The borrowed loss shrinks. Even though my mother's words were never foreign to me. All of them entered the child's language. In my language, where it will remain forever. In which, for some reason, you can simply say: 'My mum is dead.'

Everything that happened between me and my mother happened for all eternity, I realise that now. Still, this statement seems to get lost in its own profundity.

EPILOGUE

My psychiatrist has started training in psychodynamic psycho-therapy.

'According to the psychoanalytic interpretation, the father figure tends to hold more significance the less often he appears in the story.'

'But that's not the case for me, right?'

A fairy tale about mourning

A long, long time ago, behind seven graves, behind seven years, behind seven regrets

There was a girl without a mother and without fingernails, a Disney princess.

And even though she was in mourning, she was terribly happy.

And even though she lived as an orphan, she was terrible.

And even though she was motherless, she lived, terribly.

And even though she lived terribly.

And even though she lived.

I'm cleaning out my mother's closets. Only now. Two and a half years after her death. And so I find that she kept dozens of yolks from Kinder Surprises in the drawer next to her bed. She had to have eaten all the chocolate herself. All that was left of her was the toy's saffron packaging. Did she check what was inside? Didn't she know that the chocolate could be purchased separately, without any surprises? Did she remember that my stepfather bought me a surprise egg each time he went to the liquor store? And that there were entire collections of surprise toys on the shelves in my room? I was drowning in these scrambled eggs. One toy for each trip for vodka. It was our mother's remorse. But maybe it wasn't like that at all. After all, she could only afford sweets for her children for three months before her company went bankrupt. And why doesn't my daughter eat the chocolate from the surprise eggs, but instead fishes out the toys? Does she leave the chocolate for her deceased grandmother? Will almost every detail of reality continue to torment me? Entice me? She's dead, I know, but these eggs don't need to remind me of that. Or maybe they have to? Maybe if I'm not careful, it will be as if my mother never existed. One day I'll stop paying attention and lose her. That's why these thoughts race. They catch anything. Like it wasn't me. Although it wasn't anyone else either. Which came first: the chicken or the egg?

Thy will be done,
    On egg as it is in heaven

And at the very end, she said, 'Egg.'

 **MUNKEN**

Learn more about the paper we use:

www.arcticpaper.com

Arctic Paper UK Ltd
8 St Thomas Street
London
SE1 9RS